KT-227-699

# CHRISTMAS AT HORSESHOE BEND

Kentuckian gunfighter Jack Stone rides into Horseshoe Bend anticipating a peaceful Christmas with his old Army padre. But he finds that Leroy Cheney, and the notorious Inglis gang, have been terrorising the town's citizens from whom they are extracting tribute. The marshal is helpless — law and order have broken down. Suddenly an itinerant Texas cowboy arrives and provokes a confrontation. And as Jack sides with him, Leroy Cheney discovers they don't come any tougher or deadlier than Stone.

J. D. KINCAID

# CHRISTMAS AT HORSESHOE BEND

*Complete and Unabridged*

LINFORD
*Leicester*

First published in Great Britain in 2007 by
Robert Hale Limited
London

First Linford Edition
published 2009
by arrangement with
Robert Hale Limited
London

British Library CIP Data

Kincaid, J. D.
 Christmas at Horseshoe Bend.—Large print ed.—
Linford western library
 1. Western stories
 2. Large type books
 I. Title
 823.9′14 [F]

ISBN 978–1–84782–509–4

Published by
F. A. Thorpe (Publishing)
Anstey, Leicestershire

Set by Words & Graphics Ltd.
Anstey, Leicestershire
Printed and bound in Great Britain by
T. J. International Ltd., Padstow, Cornwall

This book is printed on acid-free paper

# 1

The sun beat down out of a cloudless blue sky on that glorious June day in the year of Our Lord 1884. All should have been right with the world. But in the small cattle town of Horseshoe Bend, in Moose County, Montana, all was not right. In fact, nothing had been right since Luke Chambers had sold the Black Stallion saloon to the dude from Chicago, Leroy Cheney, back in the spring. A couple of weeks after Cheney's arrival in town, his cousin, Jake Inglis, had ridden in. And Inglis had brought with him six of the roughest, toughest *hombres* ever to enter the state of Montana. Now, aided and abetted by his cousin and his gang, Leroy Cheney controlled Horseshoe Bend with an iron hand, extracting tribute from its citizens and from the homesteaders who lived just outside the town. Some had at first refused to pay and had suffered the consequences. Only Coyote Kate Driscoll still held out.

Coyote Kate was so named on account of the long, scruffy coat of coyote skins, which she wore during the winter months. Not that she looked particularly elegant during the rest of the year. With her dark-brown hair cut short beneath a large, battered, work-stained Stetson, her small, slim body covered by a voluminous and shapeless check shirt, her slender legs encased in a pair of baggy denim trousers and her feet in well-worn brown leather boots, she presented a distinctly unglamorous and unfeminine sight. Her face was oval-shaped with bright blue eyes, a small turned-up nose dusted with freckles and a wide, generous mouth. Kate might have been considered pretty had she not tended to wear a perpetual scowl and keep most of her face hidden in the shadow of the Stetson's wide, floppy brim.

The scowl was understandable, for the girl had suffered more than her fair share of hard knocks during her seventeen years. Her mother had died in childbirth when she was only six years old. The child was stillborn and this, allied to his wife's death, had proved too much for her father. He had taken to drink and, had it not been for the half-breed wrangler he employed, his horse ranch on the outskirts of Horseshoe Bend would surely have foundered. As it was, when Kate was old enough she had helped the wrangler with the horses and, at the same time, taken care of her increasingly dissolute father. Three years back the wrangler had had enough and left and then, six months later, Kate's father, drunk as a skunk, had fallen from his horse and broken his neck. Since then Kate had managed the horse ranch single-handed.

On that particular baking-hot afternoon Kate was busily engaged in grooming a splendid chestnut stallion, which she had high hopes of selling to Vince James, owner of the nearby Bar J ranch. She was performing this task in the shadow of one of her two barns when the thunder of fast-approaching horses' hoofs made her look up. What she saw caused her blood to run cold. No fewer than seven masked riders were heading towards the ranch.

Kate did not carry a handgun, but she kept a shotgun in the ranch house. Quickly, she abandoned what she was doing and ran towards the house. But she was too late. Before she could reach it, the leader of the seven rode between her and her goal. He pulled out a Colt Peacemaker and aimed it at the girl.

'Jest you stop where you are!' he rasped. 'Else I'm gonna shoot you dead.'

Coyote Kate stumbled to a halt. She was pale-faced and trembling.

'Whaddya want?' she cried.

'Whaddya think? Your hosses, of course.'

Kate stared at the seven. They had all

pulled up their kerchiefs to cover the lower half of their faces. Yet she knew exactly who they were, namely Jake Inglis and his gang.

'You sonsofbitches, leave my hosses alone!' she cried.

'Or you'll do what?' enquired the leader, Inglis, with a sneer.

This brought forth guffaws of laughter from the rest of the gang.

'I . . . I'll kill you!' By now Kate was trembling as much with rage as with fear.

'I don't take kindly to that kinda threat,' snarled Inglis menacingly, and he turned to address the others. 'OK, boys, drive off them hosses while I teach this li'l hellcat a lesson.'

'No! Stop! You cain't — '

Kate's cries were cut short as Jake Inglis leant down and dealt her a vicious blow with the barrel of his Colt Peacemaker. Fortunately, she ducked and the blow aimed at her face struck her on the top of her head. It was cushioned to some extent by the girl's

Stetson. Yet she was still knocked to the ground.

As Kate lay there semi-conscious, Inglis dismounted and proceeded to deliver a series of kicks. Two were aimed at the girl's head, but she managed to block both with her forearms. A further two struck her in the ribs, cracking one and badly bruising others.

'OK, I guess that'll do,' said Inglis, as he stood astride the softly moaning, near-senseless girl.

He slipped the revolver back into its holster and remounted his horse. Then he set off in pursuit of his gang, who, having released Coyote Kate's horses from their corral, were by now herding them out on to the plain. On his way, Inglis rounded up the splendid chestnut stallion that Kate had been grooming. Only her ancient nag, a grey mare which Kate used to pull her buckboard, remained. Hers was now a horse ranch without horses.

It was some little time before Kate

recovered her senses enough to sit up. She cried out from the pain caused by her cracked and bruised ribs. Rising to her feet was not easy. Her head swam and she sobbed as spasms of pain racked her. She staggered across towards the ranch house and grabbed hold of the hitching-rail outside it for support. Leaning against the rail, the girl slowly began to recover. Her head cleared and the pain seemed rather less intense. She looked at the empty corral and then out across the plain, where her herd of horses was almost out of sight. Tears poured uncontrollably in a constant stream down Kate's cheeks as she considered her situation. After all the years of hard work she had put in to keep the horse ranch going, it was snuffed out in a matter of minutes on that hot June afternoon. And there was no way she could afford to restock it.

But Kate was no quitter. She wiped away the tears and determined to head into town and report the matter to Marshal Bill Murray.

Hitching the nag to the buckboard was no easy task given the condition of Kate's ribs. The slightest movement caused her pain and climbing up on to the buckboard took its toll. Kate was ashen-faced and breathing heavily by the time she was sitting on the box with the reins in her hands. She sat for some minutes to let the pain subside. Then, when she felt a little better, the girl flicked the reins and urged the old grey mare forward. The nag set off at a sedate pace, for which Kate was duly thankful. She could not have handled a more mettlesome horse.

Even so, the short ride into town required all of Coyote Kate's considerable grit and determination to complete. She was clearly suffering badly by the time she drew up in front of Horseshoe Bend's law office. The short, stocky figure of Marshal Bill Murray was occupying a rocking-chair on the stoop outside and he was enjoying a cheroot. Murray was in his early forties, a decent family man. He had kept law and order pretty well until the arrival of Leroy Cheney and his associates. However, he was no match for the Inglis gang and had perforce agreed to turn a blind eye to Cheney's protection racket. He did his best, though, to save Horseshoe Bend's citizens from being harassed by the gang. He needed his job as marshal to feed his family. And Leroy Cheney needed him to remain in post so as not to alert the county sheriff to the fact that the law in Horseshoe Bend was pretty well nonexistent. Coyote Kate viewed the marshal with an appraising eye. She noted the weather-beaten features and sad brown eyes, the neat grey city-style suit and derby hat. He looked both honest and dependable. As someone who spent almost all of her time outside the town limits, Kate did not realize to what extent he had lost control of the town. Leroy Cheney had demanded tribute from her, but she didn't know who else had been threatened.

Bill Murray glanced across at the girl and removed the cheroot from between his lips.

'Howdy, Coyote,' he greeted her. 'You wantin' somethin'?'

'Yeah, Marshal, I do. I want you to arrest that dirty, thievin' skunk, Jake Inglis, an' his no-good pals for rustlin' my hosses.'

'Wa'al now, Coyote, that's a mighty serious accusation to make,' said the marshal.

'It sure is,' said another voice.

Kate glanced to the marshal's right. The tall, elegant figure of Leroy Cheney had pushed open the batwing doors of the Black Stallion saloon and stepped out on to the stoop. He strolled along the sidewalk and halted beside the lawman.

Cheney cut a handsome figure. Dark-haired, with a bold, aristocratic-looking countenance and a neat pencil-thin moustache, Cheney wore a black Prince Albert coat, a white linen shirt and bootlace tie, and a bottle-green velvet vest. He did not wear a holster, but carried a long-barrelled .30 calibre Colt in a shoulder-rig beneath his coat.

'Did you set 'em up to do it?' demanded the girl.

Cheney smiled broadly.

'Now why in tarnation would I do that?' he asked.

''Cause I refused to pay you any goddam tribute.'

'I was merely offerin' you my protection.'

'Against what?'

'Why, against the kinda misfortune you've experienced. If'n Cousin Jake an' the boys had been keepin' an eye on your place, they'd've been there to see off them hoss-rustlers.'

'They *was* the goddam hoss-rustlers!' exploded Coyote Kate.

'That ain't possible. Three of the boys are attendin' a li'l business for me on the far side of the county, while Jake an' the rest have been playin' cards in my saloon all afternoon,' said Cheney.

'Oh, yeah?'

'There are witnesses to that?' enquired the marshal.

'Sure, Bill,' said Cheney. 'Half a

11

dozen or more.'

'The bartenders an' the sportin' women who work for you?' said Kate.

'That's right.'

'But nobody else?'

'You implyin' that they ain't reliable?'

'You're darned right I am.'

'Wa'al, I don't take too kindly to bein' called a hoss-rustler,' rasped Jake Inglis, pushing open the batwing doors of the Black Stallion saloon and stepping along the sidewalk to join his cousin.

'You stinkin', lyin', thievin' sonofabitch, you — ' began Kate.

'You see the faces of the fellers who stole your hosses?' demanded Inglis.

'You know I didn't!' exclaimed Kate. 'You was all wearin' masks!'

Jake Inglis turned to the marshal.

'Y'see, Marshal, Coyote is jest jumpin' to conclusions. If'n she didn't see the rustlers' faces — '

'I know it was you, damn you!' cried Kate furiously.

Inglis's brow darkened and an angry

scowl split his ugly features. He was tall, like Leroy Cheney, but much bigger. Indeed, he was built like a bear. He crossed the stoop outside the law office, his huge fists clenched. He had thought the beating he had given the girl at the horse ranch would have been enough to subdue her indomitable spirit. But evidently it had not been sufficient, so he would just have to teach her another lesson.

By this time, the confrontation between Coyote Kate and the two cousins had attracted a small crowd of townsfolk. From the midst of these strode the tall, burly figure of Horse-shoe Bend's pastor, the Reverend Daniel Dunwoody.

'You stay just where you are!' he yelled, pointing a finger at the bearlike Jake Inglis.

The big man halted and glared at the pastor.

'You keep outa this, Reverend. 'Tain't none of your business,' he hissed.

'Well, I'm making it my business,'

retorted Dunwoody. 'From what I gather, Miss Driscoll has lost her horses to rustlers and, from the look of her, has been badly beaten. What she needs is Doc Shaw's ministrations rather than another beating at your hands.'

Inglis opened his mouth to protest, but, before he could do so, Marshal Bill Murray intervened.

'The Reverend's right,' he said. 'I can understand you bein' angry at bein' falsely accused, Jake, but — '

'He ain't falsely accused, the no-account critter!' expostulated Kate.

'There's only your word against his,' said Murray. 'That ain't no real evidence, 'specially as you didn't see the rustlers' faces. It's nuthin' I can act upon.'

'So, you ain't gonna arrest him?'

'No, Coyote, I ain't.' Murray turned to face the Reverend Daniel Dunwoody. 'Take her across to Doc Shaw's surgery. Now,' he stated firmly.

'Come along, Kate,' said Dunwoody, gently taking hold of the girl's arm.

14

'Let's go see the doc.'

As he spoke, the small, bald-headed, bespectacled figure of Doc Shaw picked his way through the crowd and took the girl's other arm.

'OK, Coyote, you've had your say. There's nuthin' more you can do here, so I figure it's time I had a good look at you,' he murmured.

The girl's shoulders slumped, she nodded sadly and, aided by the two men, limped off in the direction of the surgery.

On the stoop, Jake Inglis turned to his cousin.

'I don't think we've heard the last of that li'l hellcat,' he remarked.

'Leave her be,' said Marshal Bill Murray quietly.

'Or you'll do what?' sneered Inglis.

'Jest leave her be,' repeated the marshal.

Leroy Cheney nodded and put a hand on Inglis's shoulder.

'Enough's enough,' he said. 'Coyote Kate can rant as much as she likes, but she cain't prove or do nuthin'. So, come on, let's go have us a beer. You comin', Marshal?'

Bill Murray shook his head. He was not particularly proud of himself and he had no wish to drink with either Leroy Cheney or his ruffianly cousin. While the other two retreated inside the saloon, he resumed his seat on the rocking-chair and lit a fresh cheroot.

Meantime, the Reverend Daniel Dunwoody waited outside Doc Shaw's surgery while the doctor treated the girl's injuries. He discussed the incident with Fred Newton, the editor and proprietor of the Horseshoe Bend *Chronicle*. Newton was small and white-haired and had produced the *Chronicle* for the best part of thirty years. Like everybody else in and around Horseshoe Bend, he had been forced to pay Leroy Cheney protection money. Since he had no wish to have his press smashed and his newspaper put out of business, he had reluctantly complied with Cheney's demands. But he didn't like it. Nor did he like having Cheney censor the contents of his newspaper.

'We gotta git rid of Leroy Cheney an' his gang of pistol-packin' lunkheads,' he concluded, just as Coyote Kate and Doc Shaw reappeared.

'I've strapped her up as best I can,' said Doc Shaw. 'As far as I can ascertain, Kate's got one broken rib and several badly bruised, besides which — '

'Aw, put a sock in it, Doc!' said Kate. 'The Reverend an' Mr Newton don't wanta hear a catalogue of my cuts an' bruises. But thanks for strappin' me up. I'll be fine an' dandy now.'

She turned and, wincing, made as though to descend from the sidewalk into the street.

'Where do you think you're going?' asked Dunwoody.

'Home,' said Kate tersely.

'But, with all your horses gone . . . '

'I ain't gonna let that stinkin' sonofabitch Cheney force me off my land. I'll git by.'

'How?'

'I dunno. But I will,' said Kate, with grim determination.

'Well, just for now, come back home with me. We've got plenty of room, and Hannah and the children will be pleased to have you. You could stay until your ribs are healed.'

Kate shook her head.

'No thanks, Reverend. I gotta be goin'. Things to do.'

'At least join us for supper. Hannah makes a mean beef stew.'

Kate hesitated. She had had no lunch and was pretty hungry. She was sorely tempted.

'Accept the Reverend's offer, Coyote,' said Fred Newton. 'A good meal an' a night's rest is jest what the doctor ordered. Ain't that so, Doc?'

'Certainly is,' agreed Doc Shaw. 'Those things you've gotta do. They can surely wait until tomorrow?'

'I s'pose.'

'Come along, then,' said Dunwoody.

'OK.' Kate smiled up at the pastor. 'I ain't stayin' though. After I've eaten, I'm goin' home,' she declared.

'Very well.' Dunwoody smiled back.

They headed along the sidewalk in the direction of Dunwoody's house, which stood on the edge of town, across the street from the small wooden church.

As they approached it, the girl remarked quietly, 'This is darned good of you, Reverend. I mean, it ain't as if I ever attend your church.'

'No, though perhaps you may in the future?'

'I don't believe in no God.'

'But perhaps He believes in you. And He is the God Who likes to help those who help themselves.'

'Hmm. I ain't makin' no promises.'

'I don't expect you to. And this meal is not conditional on your joining my flock.'

'Glad to hear it.'

The Reverend Daniel Dunwoody grinned. Coyote Kate Driscoll was nothing if not honest.

# 2

Six months had passed since the raid on Coyote Kate's horse ranch. It was Monday, 22 December, and all of Montana lay under several inches of snow.

Jack Stone urged his bay gelding forward along the trail leading to Horseshoe Bend. The Kentuckian had spent some months hunting in the Sapphire Mountains west of Anaconda and now was heading south to warmer climes. But, *en route*, he intended stopping off and spending Christmas with his old Army padre at Horseshoe Bend. He had a long-standing invitation, going back to the days when they had served together in the same Union regiment during the Civil War.

Big and rugged-looking in his grey Stetson and bearskin coat, which he wore over his knee-length buckskin jacket and denim pants, Jack Stone had, in his time, been many things: deputy US marshal, sheriff, wrangler, cowboy and Army scout. He had survived the Civil War and the violent years succeeding it, and was quite definitely not a man to cross. However, for the present, he was looking to spend a pleasant, peaceful Christmas with his old buddy and his family.

As he proceeded deeper into Moose County and drew nearer to his destination, Stone heard the sound of a horse's hoofs coming up fast behind him. No snow had fallen for a little while and that which covered the trail was hard-packed, allowing the rider to maintain a fair gallop. He sped past the Kentuckian with a cheery 'Good day' and a friendly wave. Someone in a hurry to find shelter and food and drink, thought Stone. He grinned. The idea of a warming slug of whiskey encouraged him to pick up the pace. The gelding broke into a fast trot.

Ahead of the Kentuckian, the other

rider galloped on his merry way. Pete Redford was a twenty-one-year-old Texan, who had been working for a year or more on a Montana ranch. The approaching Christmas had brought back memories of home, and the urge to return to the Lone Star State had caused him to call it a day and head south. There was no chance that he would be home for Christmas, but he hoped to reach Texas early in the New Year.

Pete Redford was a handsome young fellow, tall and blond, with a pair of bright brown eyes, an engaging, youthful countenance, a ready smile and a zest for life. He was clad in the usual cowboy's attire: grey Stetson, check shirt, brown leather vest, denim pants and brown leather boots, but most of these were hidden beneath his long brown leather coat. Also hidden beneath the coat was his Colt Peacemaker, a weapon he rarely used, for he was no gunfighter.

A chill wind blew down Horseshoe Bend's Main Street, and there were few folk about when Pete Redford eventually crossed the town limits and rode into the settlement. The roofs of the town's one hotel, two saloons and various shops, stores and houses were liberally coated with snow. Main Street itself, however, had been churned up by horses and wagons and was mostly mud, with only a few patches of snow here and there on its fringes.

The cowboy slackened his pace. It was late afternoon and would soon be dark. He was on the lookout, therefore, for somewhere to stay the night. He spotted the Horseshoe Bend Hotel, noting that it stood next to Flanagan's saloon, with the town's other saloon, Leroy Cheney's Black Stallion, on the opposite side of the street. Redford had the same thought that had struck the Kentuckian out on the trail. Before booking a room for the night, he would warm himself with a few slugs of whiskey. He rode across to Flanagan's saloon and dismounted.

While Redford was engaged in

hitching his piebald to the rail outside the saloon, two large, heavily built, bearded figures pushed open the batwing doors of the Black Stallion saloon and stepped out on to the stoop. Hal and Nat Rogers were brothers. Hal, the elder, was an inch or two taller than Nat. Both were mean-minded, ugly customers, and each carried a Remington in his holster. They had ridden into town with Jake Inglis and were enjoying lording it over its citizens.

They glanced up and down the street. Two cowpokes from the Bar J ranch were loading supplies on to a buckboard in front of Sid Harrison's general store, as was Coyote Kate Driscoll. Norman Black, proprietor of the Horseshoe Bend Hotel, was crossing the street on his way to the barbering parlour, while a couple of women were coming out of Lettie Crichton's drygoods store. Otherwise Main Street was deserted.

'You know what to do, boys,' said

Leroy Cheney from the doorway of his saloon.

Standing beside Cheney, his cousin grinned and added, 'Give the feller a chance before dustin' him up.'

The brothers nodded and, descending from the stoop, made their way across the muddy thoroughfare to where Pete Redford had hitched his horse to the rail and was preparing to ascend the short flight of wooden steps leading up to Flanagan's saloon.

'Hey, you!' rasped Hal Rogers.

Redford turned round.

'You addressin' me?' he demanded.

Although by nature easy-going, the young Texan was riled by the other's aggressive tone.

' 'Course I'm addressin' you,' said Hal Rogers. 'You're evidently a stranger in these parts.'

'So?'

'So, I'm gonna give you a li'l advice. Don't go drinkin' in that there saloon.'

'No. Cross the street an' use the Black Stallion,' said his brother.

'An' jest why would I do that?' enquired Redford.

' 'Cause Flanagan's beer ain't worth drinkin',' replied Hal Rogers.

'That don't matter to me. I was plannin' on drinkin' whiskey,' said Redford.

'His whiskey's rot-gut,' growled Nat Rogers.

'Yeah, wa'al, I'll jest make up my own mind 'bout that,' retorted the Texan.

'I don't think so,' said the elder of the two brothers.

It was at this moment that Marshal Bill Murray stepped outside the law office. He had been watching events develop and didn't like what he saw.

'What's goin' on?' he cried.

'Jest stay outa this, Marshal,' said Leroy Cheney.

'Yeah, we got ourselves a stranger who ain't inclined to take a li'l friendly advice,' explained Jake Inglis.

'I don't want no killin',' said Murray anxiously.

'Don't worry, Marshal. There ain't

gonna be no killin'. The boys'll merely show the stranger that it ain't altogether wise to reject their advice. Ain't that right, boys?' he yelled.

'Sure is, Jake,' said Hal Rogers.

Pete Redford felt a tremor of fear. He was no coward, but he was in a strange town and about to be set upon by a pair of roughnecks. Also, it seemed that the law, in the person of the marshal, was unlikely to intervene.

He squared up to the two brothers.

'I ain't lookin' for a fight,' he said. 'But you ain't tellin' me where I can an' cannot drink.'

'No?' said Hal Rogers, and he aimed a punch at Redford's jaw.

The young Texan ducked and rammed a right hook into Hal Rogers' belly. The big man grunted and doubled up, where-upon Redford followed up with a left hand to the jaw. This sent Hal Rogers staggering backwards. He shook his head, but did not go down.

Having got his opponent groggy, Redford went after him. He drew back his right fist, intending to deal Hal Rogers a knockout blow. However, he found his arm grabbed by Nat Rogers, who, at the same time, dealt him a chopping blow to the back of his neck. Redford dropped on to his knees in the mud and, laughing harshly, Nat Rogers lashed out with his boot and kicked the cowboy hard in the kidneys. Redford cried out and fell forward. He stuck out his hands, to prevent himself falling face downwards in the quag-mire that was Main Street, and found that he was staring at the boot of the elder brother, only inches from his nose.

Hal Rogers aimed a tremendous kick at Redford's head, which the Texan just managed to dodge by twisting quickly sideways. He pushed himself upright and hastily raised his fists. As he did so, Nat Rogers stepped up behind him and grabbed him in a bear hug. Redford struggled to free himself, but could not break loose from the other's vicelike grip. Consequently, he was quite unable to defend himself against Hal Rogers's next attack.

A vicious grin spread across Hal Rogers's ugly features as he stepped up and prepared to smash the cowboy's face into a pulp. He drew back his fist and was just about to deliver the first punch when a voice behind him shouted, 'You hit him one more time an' I'll shoot your goddam head off!'

Hal Rogers whirled round, to find Coyote Kate standing up in her buckboard and aiming her shotgun at his head. Since the incident in June when she had lost all of her horses, Kate had taken to keeping the shotgun with her at all times. And there was no doubting that she had every intention of firing it.

Hal Rogers backed off, while his brother released the young Texan and stepped away. Both gazed anxiously at the grim-faced seventeen-year-old. Neither fancied receiving a blast of ten-gauge shot.

From his position on the stoop in

front of the Black Stallion saloon, Jake Inglis shouted, 'Put down that gun, Coyote, else you're liable to git yourself killed!' Behind him, the rest of his gang had appeared, each and every one of them clutching a revolver and ready to shoot. There was Red Burton, tall, rake-thin and carrot-haired, an evil gleam in his coal-black eyes; Timmy Tinker, short, squat and bewhiskered, ever eager to start shooting; Roscoe Jonson, rough, tough and with the temper of an angry grizzly; and Roy Davin, a bearded giant of a man, whose huge fist made the Colt Peacemaker he was clutching look like a mere toy. All four of them would have quite happily gunned down the girl.

'I . . . I said I don't want no killin',' cried a nervous Marshal Bill Murray.

'And there isn't going to be any,' announced the Reverend Daniel Dunwoody, who, together with Fred Newton, Doc Shaw, Norman Black the hotelier, Ben Brady the mortician, and several other of Horseshoe Bend's citizens had gathered to see what was going on.

'Now, you keep outa this, Reverend!' rasped Inglis.

'Yes. Your job is to save the souls of sinners, not the lives of fools,' interjected Cheney.

'Mebbe the Reverend can persuade Coyote to put down the shotgun?' suggested the marshal.

'I'll see what I can do, Bill,' said Dunwoody and, turning to Kate, he remarked, 'It's OK. The fight's over. I'll tend to this young feller.'

'Wa'al . . . '

'Step aside, boys,' said Dunwoody. 'You can leave the stranger in my care.'

'He ain't goin' into Flanagan's saloon,' growled Hal Rogers truculently, although still with an anxious eye trained on Coyote Kate.

Dunwoody glanced towards the saloon, where Sam Flanagan, a red-faced, bright-eyed Irishman, stood peering over the batwing doors and watching events unroll. He badly needed customers, yet he had no wish that the young stranger should get himself killed for preferring his to Leroy Cheney's saloon. He opened his mouth to say as much, but was forestalled by the arrival in town of Jack Stone.

The Kentuckian had ridden in while the confrontation between Pete Redford and the Rogers brothers was taking place. Spotting his old Army padre, the Reverend Daniel Dunwoody, Stone called out, 'Howdy, Reverend, what in tarnation's goin' on around here?'

Dunwoody whirled round, a wide smile splitting his handsome features as he recognized the Kentuckian.

'Wa'al, after all these years, if it ain't my old comrade, Jack Stone!' he exclaimed. Then he replied to Stone's question. 'Jest experiencing a little local difficulty, Jack But I reckon it's about over. Isn't it, Mr Cheney?'

Leroy Cheney frowned.

'That depends on him,' he said, pointing at the Texan.

Stone dismounted and began hitching his bay gelding to the rail next to

Redford's piebald.

'So,' he said, addressing Redford, 'can you explain what's goin' on, for I missed the beginnin' of all this?'

'These two lunkheads seem determined I don't enter that there saloon,' replied the young cowboy, indicating the two brothers who were still barring his way.

'Is that a fact?' said Stone.

'It is,' growled Hal Rogers.

'We was advisin' him to drink across the street at the Black Stallion,' added Nat Rogers.

'But you rejected that advice?' said Stone.

'I sure did,' said Redford.

Stone grinned and began walking towards Flanagan's saloon. As he approached the foot of the flight of wooden steps leading up on to the stoop, Nat Rogers stepped in front of him.

'Where d'you think you're goin'?' enquired the gunslinger.

Stone pushed him aside and began to

mount the steps.

'I'm gonna git me a drink,' he said.

'Not in Flanagan's, you ain't!' yelled Nat Rogers.

He clattered up the steps in pursuit of Stone, who, upon reaching the stoop, turned abruptly and grabbed the other by his shirt-front. Nat Rogers was no lightweight, yet the big Kentuckian heaved him clean off his feet and hurled him backwards, to land with a tremendous squelch in the quagmire that was Main Street. Mud splattered all ways, most of it speckling Hal Rogers.

He glanced down at the dazed, gasping figure of his younger brother and a furious scowl suffused his ugly features. He grabbed the Colt Peacemaker from its holster. But he was too late. It had barely cleared leather when, on looking up, he found himself staring into the muzzle of Jack Stone's Frontier Model Colt.

'Toss that gun behind you,' said Stone. 'An' do it nice an' slow.'

There was no denying the menace in

the Kentuckian's voice and, while Hal Rogers might not have been the smartest man in Horseshoe Bend, he was certainly not stupid enough to defy Stone. Reluctantly, he threw the revolver several feet behind him. From his vantage point on the stoop, Stone smiled. But there was no laughter in his pale-blue eyes.

'Now, come up here,' he rasped.

Hal Rogers stepped round his fallen brother and slowly approached the steps. There was fear in his eyes as he began to mount them. Like most bullies, he was a coward at heart.

As he clambered on to the stoop, Stone swifty reversed the frontier Model Colt and struck Hal Rogers a fearsome blow with the barrel. It struck Rogers across the bridge of his nose, smashing it and sending him tumbling to the foot of the steps. His mud-splattered body sprawled there, quite motionless, his face a crimson mask. A few feet away, Nat Rogers remained still in a semiconscious state.

Both brothers were, without question, *hors de combat*.

Across the street, Jake Inglis snarled, 'OK, boys, let's go git the sonofabitch!'

'No! I won't allow it!' cried Marshal Bill Murray.

Inglis laughed harshly.

'You won't allow it!' he exclaimed contemptuously. 'How are you gonna stop us, Marshal; tell me that?'

Murray turned to Leroy Cheney and said imploringly, 'For God's sake, Leroy, d'you want a massacre on your hands? You've got the town in your pocket, but you let Jake an' his boys loose an' you could jeopardize everythin'. An' for what? Jest to prevent a coupla strangers, who will probably have moved on by tomorrow, from havin' theirselves a drink at Flanagan's.'

'This could set a precedent.'

'Aw, come on, Leroy!'

Leroy Cheney considered the matter and, ever the pragmatist, decided there was some sense in the marshal's words.

'OK. Let's do nuthin' stupid. Jake,

you, me an' the marshal will adjourn to talk this over.'

'What about Hal an' Nat?' demanded Inglis.

'Git the rest of your boys to carry 'em back here to the saloon. An' they can also fetch Doc Shaw to patch 'em up.'

Jake Inglis nodded. Although eager to avenge the two brothers, he recognized his cousin's astuteness and was, therefore, inclined to bow to his judgement. So far, doing just that had paid off handsomely.

On the opposite side of the street, Sam Flanagan flung open the batwing doors and stepped out on to the stoop.

'You fellers comin' in?' he asked.

'Sure thing,' said Stone.

'You betcha,' said Pete Redford.

'Would you care to join us, Reverend?' enquired the Kentuckian.

Dunwoody smiled wryly.

'I don't usually frequent bar-rooms,' he confessed. 'However, on this occasion, I shall make an exception.'

'I'm comin', too!' cried Coyote Kate,

scrambling down off the buckboard and hurrying towards the saloon.

Pete Redford turned and watched the small figure approach, still clutching her shotgun.

'Thanks for helpin' out, young feller,' said Redford.

'I ain't no feller!' retorted Kate. 'I'm a girl.'

The Texan executed a quick double-take, noting the pretty little face half-hidden beneath the large, floppy-brimmed Stetson.

'S . . . sorry,' he stammered. 'The hat an' the coyote-skin coat fooled me. I can see now that you're a girl.'

'That's OK.' Kate grinned and stuck out her right hand. 'Kate Driscoll,' she said.

'Pete Redford,' he responded, shaking the girl's hand.

They followed the Kentuckian and the pastor into the saloon. And, as they vanished inside, Jake Inglis's four gun-slingers picked up the two Rogers brothers and bore them off towards the Black Stallion.

# 3

Flanagan's saloon was like a hundred others in small townships across the West. It consisted of a large, rectangular bar-room, with brass lamps hanging from the rafters and the floor spread with sawdust. There were several tables and chairs scattered across its length and breadth, and the bar itself, with its mahogany bar-top, stood at the far end. Sam Flanagan had retired behind the bar, ready and anxious to serve his customers. They, meantime, were busy introducing themselves.

Then, once these formalities were concluded, Jake Stone turned to the saloon-keeper.

'I'll have me a whiskey,' he said.

'Me, too,' added Redford.

'What about you, Reverend, an' you, miss?' Stone enquired of the other two.

'No, thanks. I don't touch strong

liquor,' said Dunwoody.

'Wa'al, the good Lord turned water into wine. So . . . ?'

'Sam doesn't serve wine.'

'No, I guess not.' Stone turned to Coyote Kate. 'What about you, miss?'

Kate shook her head.

'Nope. I don't touch strong liquor either,' she stated flatly. She had watched her father drink himself to death and had no intention of following in his footsteps. 'I don't s'pose I could have a cup of coffee, could I, Sam?' she asked wistfully.

'Yes. That would be nice,' said Dunwoody.

The saloon-keeper smiled broadly.

'Sure thing, folks,' he said. Then he turned and called through from his position behind the bar-counter to the saloon's rear quarters. 'Mary, can you bring through a coupla cups of coffee, please, for the Reverend an' Coyote?'

This message delivered, Flanagan reached for a bottle of rye whiskey and poured three generous measures, one each for Jack Stone and Pete Redford and the third for himself. The bottle he left standing on the counter.

'So, Jack, is this a chance encounter or did you come looking for me?' asked Dunwoody.

'I came lookin' for you, Reverend,' replied the Kentuckian. 'Figured I'd take you up on that invitation to spend Christmas with you here in Horseshoe Bend. If'n that's OK?'

'That's fine. It's just that you've been a long time coming.'

'Yeah. I guess this is the first time since we parted that I've been up here in Montana.'

'Well, it's nice to see you. And, if you're going to stay with me, why not drop the Reverend and call me Daniel?'

'OK, Daniel. Here's to you,' said Stone, raising his glass and knocking back a large quantity of Flanagan's red-eye.

At this moment the saloon-keeper's rosy-cheeked wife appeared, bearing two large mugs of coffee. She handed them across the counter to Dunwoody and Coyote Kate.

Stone settled up with Flanagan for the whiskeys and the coffees, and the saloon-keeper beamed, saying fervently, 'It sure is nice to have customers mid-week!'

'Yeah; what's goin' on around here?' enquired Stone.

'Wa'al, it all began back in April, when Leroy Cheney hit town. He had jest bought the Black Stallion saloon, an' he brought with him Jake Inglis an' his gang. Inglis is his cousin, by the way,' said the saloon-keeper.

'I take it Cheney's aimin' to force you outa business by scarin' off anyone who tries to enter your premises?'

'That's right. There ain't been no townsfolk nor homesteaders across this threshold since last April. Jake Inglis an' his gang have seen to that.'

'So, how have you managed to keep goin'?'

'I'm gittin' by on my Saturday night takin's. That's when the hands from the

Lazy S, the Bar J an' the High Butte ranches ride into town.'

'Inglis an' his toughs don't try to prevent the cowboys enterin' your saloon?'

'Nope.'

'Cheney is happy to terrorize the townsfolk of Horseshoe Bend, but he daren't antagonize the owners of those ranches. They are powerful men in Moose County. Anyway, the cowboys are his best customers and he'd be a fool to let Inglis and his men pick a fight with them,' explained Dunwoody.

'Guess he would at that.'

'Sam is in direct competition with Leroy Cheney, which is why Cheney is so keen to put him out of business,' said the pastor.

'He wants both saloons. 'Deed, he made me an offer for mine only a coupla weeks after he got here,' said Flanagan.

'A fair offer?' enquired Stone.

'No, it was a derisory amount he proposed to pay. I refused an' he's been blockadin' this saloon ever since.'

'But that ain't all,' interjected Coyote Kate. 'The sonofabitch is extortin' protection money from each an' every business an' homestead in an' around Horseshoe Bend.'

'Yeah,' muttered Flanagan. 'Not content with blockadin' my saloon, he's also extractin' money on threat of death if'n I don't pay up.'

'Sid Harrison, the proprietor of the town's general store, at first refused to pay this tribute,' said Dunwoody. 'Then, one dark night, he was set upon and beaten up. He never saw his attackers. He started paying after that.'

'Anyone else refuse to pay?' asked Stone.

'Yeah. Me,' said Coyote Kate.

The Kentuckian eyed the diminutive figure in the long, voluminous coyote-skin coat. She might be young and she might be tiny, he mused, but she sure as hell had guts.

'What happened?' he asked.

'Jake Inglis an' his shootists chased

off all my hosses. I ran a hoss ranch, y'see.'

'An' now?'

'I git by. I've got me a few chickens an' I grow some vegetables. I supply folks with eggs, potatoes an' beans. It ain't like runnin' a hoss ranch, but it's a livin',' said Kate. 'An' I still don't pay tribute to that no-account critter,' she added defiantly.

'What has he got to say 'bout that?'

'Nuthin'.'

'It isn't worth his while,' said Daniel Dunwoody. 'I imagine Kate earns barely enough to exist on. Besides, when Inglis chased off her horses, he also beat her up and that didn't go down too well with the marshal. It's my guess Bill Murray has warned Cheney to leave her be.'

'This town marshal of yours, is he on the take?' asked the Kentuckian.

'No. Bill Murray is a decent man. But there is no way he can take on the Inglis gang on his own.'

'Then, why don't he call in some

help?' demanded Pete Redford, entering the discussion for the first time.

'Again I'm only guessing,' said Dunwoody, 'but I expect Cheney has threatened to kill or beat up his wife and young family should the marshal make any move to contact the county sheriff.'

'That certainly puts him on the spot,' muttered Stone.

'Yeah. However, Cheney needs him so as to forestall any outside interference. So, Bill has some influence, and does his best to maintain a semblance of law and order.'

'But for how long?' rasped Flanagan. 'Since he took over the Black Stallion, Leroy Cheney has brought in several sportin' women an' is encouragin' all kinds of no-good trash into town. Unless somethin' is done soon, Horseshoe Bend will degenerate into a lawless hell-hole.'

'Yes, I fear you may be right, Sam,' averred the pastor glumly.

'Wa'al, if'n this here marshal cain't

contact the county sheriff for help, that don't mean nobody else can,' said Redford.

'Two have tried and failed,' said Dunwoody. 'Both set off for the county seat, Elk City, intending to complain to Sheriff Beau Flanders, but neither got there. One was set upon by a gang of masked men and badly beaten. Then he was lifted into the saddle and sent back the way he came. The other wasn't so fortunate. His horse trotted back into town without its rider. He was found two miles out along the trail, with a couple of bulletholes in his chest. He was stone dead.'

'Hmm. So, what had Cheney to say?' growled Stone.

'He denied that his cousin was involved and simply said that that was why folks needed to pay tribute, in order to obtain protection against bandits, rustlers and suchlike, the protection which he was offering.'

'The sonofabitch said much the same when Inglis an' his gang stole my 'hosses,' said Kate, her eyes angry and her face transfigured by a dark scowl.

'You spoke about the ranchers whose hands frequent Horseshoe Bend on Saturday nights,' said Redford. 'You said they were powerful men. Wa'al, couldn't you approach them an' ask . . . ?'

Daniel Dunwoody shook his head.

'Our then mayor, Norman Black, tried. But they weren't interested. So long as their cowpokes weren't threatened, they didn't see why they should get involved. Cheney has demanded no tribute from them. Neither, I must admit, has he demanded any from me. Perhaps Bill Murray has warned him not to. Bill is regular attender at church, you see.'

'Hmm.' Jack Stone scratched his head and finished his whiskey. He lit a cheroot and gave the matter some more thought. 'You tried wirin' the sheriff?' he asked.

'Anyone goes into the telegraph office, one of Inglis's gunslingers follows him in. It's situated almost

48

opposite the Black Stallion an', consequently, is easily kept under surveillance
by the gang,' remarked Flanagan.

'I see.'

'So, Jack, you haven't picked the best
of times to visit me here in Horseshoe
Bend,' said Dunwoody. 'Leroy Cheney
replaced Norman Black as mayor in
November in a rigged election and now
controls just about everything in town. I
fear, therefore, that this Christmas is
going to be anything but a season of
peace and goodwill to all men.'

'Mebbe I should have come last
year?' said Stone wryly.

'You should. But we shall just have to
make the most of it. What about you,
Mr Redford; are you merely passing
through?'

'That's right, Reverend,' said Redford. 'I was workin' on a ranch some
miles north of here when I suddenly got
the urge to head for home.'

'And are you aiming to spend the
night here in Horseshoe Bend?'

'I was.'

'And now?'

'Wa'al, I dunno. If'n I don't, it'll feel like I'm runnin' away from a fight.'

'This isn't your fight.' Dunwoody turned to the Kentuckian. 'And it isn't yours either, Jack,' he said. 'I am inviting you to stay to celebrate Christmas, not to get yourself killed.'

'I ain't reckonin' on gittin' myself killed, Daniel,' said Stone.

'Should you take on Leroy Cheney and his associates, you could do. Easily. Excluding Cheney himself, you'd be facing no fewer than seven professional shootists.'

'I'll bear that in mind.'

'You do that, Jack. And, as for you, Mr Redford, I would suggest you spend the night under my roof and head out of town at first light. Unless you really do want to spend Christmas here?'

'No, Reverend. I'll lam outa town at first light. But I don't intend headin' south straightaway.'

'You don't?'

'Nope. I figure I'll make a detour to your county seat, Elk City, if'n you'll give me directions,' said the Texan, adding, 'You write a letter, askin' the sheriff to investigate the goin's-on here in Horseshoe Bend, an' I'll deliver it for you.'

Dunwoody smiled gratefully at the young cowboy.

'Thank you. That could solve all our problems,' he averred.

'S'pose Leroy Cheney guesses what you're up to?' interjected Coyote Kate.

'Why in blue blazes should he?' cried Redford.

'No reason. But he might,' said the girl.

'I'll ride with Mr Redford as far as Elk City,' volunteered Stone. 'Jest to be on the safe side. Can I git there an' back in one day, Daniel?'

'I reckon so,' said Dunwoody.

'That's settled, then.' Stone addressed the saloon-keeper. 'Another coupla whiskeys. An' how about you two? Any more coffee required?'

'No thanks,' said the pastor.

'Nor for me,' said Coyote Kate.

Sam Flanagan grinned, picked up the whiskey bottle and poured Stone and the Texan another two generous slugs of the red-eye. This time he did not join them. He knew it would be easy for a saloon-keeper to drink his profits and, anyway, the way things were, he was barely breaking even.

'I jest hope an' pray that Sheriff Beau Flanders answers the Reverend's plea,' he said feelingly.

'Don't we all?' muttered Kate.

Then, as Stone and Redford lifted their glasses to their lips, the batwing doors swung open and Leroy Cheney and Marshal Bill Murray entered the bar-room. The former swaggered in, while the latter trudged in, looking a trifle shamefaced.

'Whaddya want?' rasped Flanagan, not exactly the genial host.

'Jest a li'l word with your new friends,' replied Cheney smoothly.

'Oh, yeah?'

'Yes, Sam. The marshal here has

somethin' to say. Haven't you, Bill?'

The lawman looked more uncomfortable than ever.

'Er . . . yeah, I . . . I guess so,' he stammered.

'Spit it out, then,' said Flanagan.

Bill Murray cleared his throat and then said quietly, 'I don't want no repeat of this afternoon's violence. Next time, someone could easily git hisself killed.'

'So?' Stone glowered at both him and Cheney.

'So, I'm orderin' you two strangers to hightail it outa town. Pronto.'

'There is no law that says — ' began Dunwoody.

'I'm the law round here, Reverend,' Murray interrupted him.

'Jack Stone is an old friend,' said the pastor. 'And I have invited him to stay over Christmas. As for Mr Redford, he will stay with me overnight and then set out at first light.'

'I've a long ways to go,' explained Redford.

'Wa'al . . . ' Murray shot a nervous glance towards Cheney.

Cheney, elegant and suave as ever, smiled silkily and said, 'Stayin' overnight is fine. But I feel you should insist that both of 'em leave town tomorrow mornin'. After all, we don't want no breakdown in law an' order, now do we, Marshal?'

'We sure don't,' said the marshal. 'Therefore, Mr Stone, I would ask you — '

'OK.' Stone cut the peace officer short. 'I'll ride outa town with Mr Redford. Anythin' to keep the peace.'

Leroy Cheney eyed the big, tough-looking Kentuckian with some surprise. He had not expected Bill Murray's ultimatum to be so readily accepted by Stone.

'Wa'al,' he said, 'that's mighty sensible of you.'

'So, if that's all you're wantin' . . . ?' growled Sam Flanagan.

'Yeah, I guess that's it.' Cheney smiled smugly and, clapping the marshal on the shoulder, said, 'Come on,

Bill, let's be goin'.'

'Sure ... sure thing,' muttered Murray, only too relieved that the two strangers hadn't defied his ultimatum.

Leroy Cheney swaggered out of the saloon, just as he had swaggered in, while the marshal trotted unhappily behind him.

Once they had vanished through the batwing doors, Daniel Dunwoody turned to Stone and the young Texan and said, 'OK, gentlemen, finish your drinks and we'll head for home.'

The pastor's house was only five minutes' walk away. There he introduced Jack Stone and Pete Redford to his wife, Hannah, and their two children, fourteen-year-old Paul and twelve-year-old Ruth. Hannah was small and dark in a neat blue-and-white gingham dress, Paul merry-faced and big-built like his father, and Ruth bright-eyed and petite like her mother.

Dinner that evening was a jolly affair, the two travellers tucking into Hannah's excellent roast chicken with evident relish, and both regaling Dunwoody and his family with tales of their various adventures.

At the opposite end of Horseshoe Bend, alone on her one-time ranch, Kate Driscoll was eating a lonely and rather more frugal meal. She was feeling happier, though, than at any time since losing her horses in the summer. Pete Redford's promise to deliver a letter from the Reverend Dunwoody to Sheriff Beau Flanders in Elk City had given her hope that Leroy Cheney's reign of terror might soon be at an end.

# 4

Tuesday, 23 December, dawned bitterly cold, with snow falling in large white flakes. It was not the kind of weather to tempt the citizens of Horseshoe Bend out of doors. Many took advantage of the weather to remain in rather later than usual. However, there were some who were up and about early. The Reverend Daniel Dunwoody was one such person.

He sat in his study carefully composing his letter to the county sheriff. He kept it brief and to the point, and had just completed it when his two guests came down for breakfast.

''Mornin', fellers. How did you sleep?' he asked.

'Jest fine,' said Stone.

'Like a log,' said Redford.

'Well, it's snowing pretty heavily. Perhaps you should delay your departure until it stops?'

Stone shook his head.

'No, Daniel, we don't want no confrontation with the marshal, certainly not here in your home.'

'That's right,' agreed Redford. 'We said we'd go. So, let's jest do that. Have you written that letter for the sheriff?'

'Yes. Here it is.' Dunwoody handed the letter to the cowboy and then turned to Stone. 'Will you return here like you originally planned, Jack?' he enquired.

'No, I'll head on south like I promised the marshal. Probably ride a ways with Pete,' said Stone. 'I'm sorry I won't be spendin' Christmas with you an' your family, Daniel, but I feel it's best I don't'

The Kentuckian had no wish to duck a fight, yet he realized that, should he return to Horseshoe Bend, he would surely be putting the pastor and his family in danger. It was better to ride on and leave Sheriff Beau Flanders and his deputies to restore law and order to the town.

And so it was that, following a hearty breakfast, Stone and the cowboy saddled up and took their leave of Dunwoody, Hannah and their two children. They cantered through the fast-falling snow, back along Main Street towards the point where they could pick up the trail that would lead them south. According to Dunwoody, Elk City lay ten miles away to the west. The trail split four miles outside Horseshoe Bend, one fork continuing on southward, while the other led westward to the county seat. The detour to Elk City would not, they considered, delay their journey south by more than a few hours.

The two men did not ride out of town unnoticed. As they cantered past the Black Stallion, Jake Inglis peered out of the saloon's window and watched them go. He turned to his cousin, who was sitting at a table drinking coffee and smoking a large cigar.

'Wa'al, Leroy, there they go,' he said.

Leroy Cheney smiled slyly.

'I s'pose Hal an' Nat will be in place by now?' he murmured.

'You can bet your bottom dollar they will,' replied Inglis.

'I jest hope they ain't frozen solid out there.'

'Yeah.'

'You told 'em to stage their ambush some ways along the fork leadin' to Elk City?'

'I did.'

'Good! If them fellers continue on south, I don't want the brothers bushwhackin' 'em. We don't want no killin's unless they're absolutely necessary.'

'You figure they will head south?'

'I dunno, Jake. They might, or mebbe they'll head on into Elk City an' brief the sheriff 'bout what's goin' on here. An' we cain't afford for that to happen.'

'Hal an' Nat will make darned sure it don't. Hell, they're real anxious to take revenge on that pal of the Reverend!'

'That's what bothers me. This ain't

about revenge. This is about stoppin' word gittin' to the sheriff. Killin' is a last resort. Too many deaths an' the sheriff is liable to investigate anyway.'

'Don't worry, Leroy. I gave the brothers strict instructions, an' they ain't stupid enough to disobey, believe me. Also, I told 'em, if'n they do bushwhack them fellers, to make sure they hide corpses, saddles, everythin', an' then take their hosses an' sell 'em to Trader Tomkins. He's a man who asks no questions.'

Cheney nodded. He wouldn't have trusted the Rogers brothers not to disobey *his* instructions, but he felt confident they would stick to his cousin's directive.

And he was right. When, an hour earlier, Hal and Nat Rogers had set out, Jake Inglis instructed them to do nothing to hinder Stone and Redford's passage should they decide to head south. This hadn't pleased the two brothers. However, they had gone along with this edict and now were crouching half way up the lee side of a hill, one quarter of a mile past the fork in the trail. From here they could just make out, through the curtain of falling snow, the spot where the trail divided.

'I sure as hell hope those two bastards *don't* head south,' muttered Hal Rogers, his teeth chattering as he crouched in the saddle and waited. His broken nose was swollen and sore, and he was desperate to kill the man who had inflicted that gruesome injury.

'If they do ride this way, I'm gonna take the Reverend's buddy. You aim for the younger feller, OK?' he said.

'Yup,' was Nat Rogers's monosyllabic response.

Covered from head to foot in snow, he prayed that they would not have too long to wait. He wore fur mitts, which he had plunged deep into the pockets of his bearskin coat. Even so, he was afraid his hands would become so numb that, when the moment came, he would be unable to handle his Winchester.

At the same time that Jack Stone and

Pete Redford were riding out of Horseshoe Bend and the Rogers brothers were lying in ambush along the fork to Elk City, Kate Driscoll was saddling her old grey mare. The seventeen-year-old had passed a restless night troubled by bad dreams, the last of which had featured the Kentuckian and the Texan lying dead in the snow. Both had been shot in the back.

Taking this as a warning sign, Kate had risen, wolfed down a quick breakfast and, wrapped in her coyote-skin coat, had hurried outside. Once she had saddled the mare, the girl rammed her shotgun into the saddle boot and hastily mounted. Her premonition that Stone and Redford would be ambushed gave impetus to her setting off through the fast-falling snow. She must prevent this at all costs, even though it meant riding through what threatened to develop into a full-scale blizzard.

Kate guessed that, if an ambush were to take place, it would be somewhere after the fork in the trail. Therefore, she needed to reach that stretch of the trail before Stone and Redford got there. And, since she suspected that they would already be on their way, she had no choice other than to take the short-cut through Wolf Pass.

This was a perfectly good route during the summer months, but, in the present wintry conditions, it could well be impassable. Kate felt she had to take that chance. She forced the mare on through the driving snow. Visibility was restricted and the girl had difficulty in following the trail. She knew, however, that, should she stray off it, the mare might easily become stuck in a snowdrift.

She pressed on, riding deeper and deeper into Wolf Pass. So far, so good; the way was still clear.

The main trail was no less difficult to negotiate. And, so as not to stray from it, Jack Stone and his young companion rode in single file, the Kentuckian leading the way.

After what seemed a veritable age, Stone eventually spotted the fork in the trail.

'There it is!' he shouted. 'We bear right here.'

'Thank God! I was scared we might miss the goddam fork altogether,' replied Redford.

'If the snow was fallin' any thicker we more'n likely would have done,' said Stone.

'Yeah. So, let's hope we reach Elk City 'fore these conditions git any worse,' muttered the young Texan.

'Amen to that!'

Stone urged on his bay gelding, while Redford followed on the piebald.

They had progressed about 300 yards beyond the fork when the blast of a shotgun rent the air. This was immediately followed by a loud scream.

Stone pulled his Winchester from the saddle boot and galloped forward. Peering through the falling snow, he could just discern the two figures huddled on the hillside to his left. One sat astride his horse, while the other was spreadeagled on the ground, having been shot clean out of the saddle.

The rider, who remained in the saddle, hurriedly brought his rifle to bear on the Kentuckian. But his numb fingers were slow to squeeze the trigger and, before he could do so, Stone fired. Once; twice; thrice. The bullets slammed into the bushwhacker's chest, sending him toppling to the ground.

As he hit the snow-covered trail, his fellow ambusher attempted to struggle to his feet. Another three shots barked forth from Stone's Winchester, knocking the ambusher flat on his back and killing him outright.

'Holy cow! That was some shootin'!' exclaimed Pete Redford.

'It sure was. I hit one of the critters an' unseated him, but unfortunately didn't kill him,' said Coyote Kate, as she emerged out of the swirling snow upon her grey mare, clutching her shotgun.

The three riders dismounted and

examined the two corpses.

'Hmm. It's them danged Rogers brothers,' stated Kate.

'Sent out here to prevent us from reachin' Elk City,' commented Redford.

'Which they would have done had it not been for you,' remarked Stone to the girl.

'Aw, shucks! I didn't do nuthin' much,' said Kate deprecatingly.

'Your shot alerted me to the fact they was lurkin' here,' said Stone.

'Yeah. How'd you know they would be lyin' in wait for us?' asked Redford.

'An' how in tarnatian did you git here? You certainly didn't follow the main trail from Horseshoe Bend,' said Stone.

'Wa'al, I didn't know it was the Rogers brothers who would be here,' replied Kate. 'But I guessed that snake in the grass, Leroy Cheney, would send someone out to lie in wait for you, jest in case you took the fork to Elk City.' Then she added, 'So, I figured I'd sneak up on 'em by way of Wolf Pass.'

The Kentuckian peered through the curtain of swirling snow. He could only just make out the outline of the mountains through which the girl had passed.

'Hell, you took one helluva risk!' he stated. 'Goddammit, you could easily have ended up in a snowdrift an' frozen to death!'

'Wa'al, I reckoned it was a risk worth takin', Mr Stone,' declared Kate.

Jack Stone smiled. The seventeen-year-old was, in his estimation, one tough little lady.

'I know we ain't long acquainted,' he said, 'but I guess this li'l adventure makes it OK for us to drop the formalities an' call each other by our Christian names. Whaddya say, Kate?'

'I s'pose it's more friendly-like,' replied the girl, with a shy smile.

'I agree. Thanks for savin' our lives, Kate,' said Pete Redford.

'Yeah, wa'al, what do we do now?' she enquired.

'Head on to Elk City,' said the Kentuckian.

'Can I ride with you?' she asked.

''Course you can,' said Stone.

'What about the Rogers brothers?' demanded Redford.

'We leave 'em be,' said Stone. 'I figure that by an' by, when they don't report back, Leroy Cheney will send someone out to look for 'em.'

'I guess,' said the young Texan.

'So, let's git goin'.'

Thereupon, they quickly remounted and set off at a canter.

The conditions remained much the same until they were less than one mile from their destination, when suddenly the falling snow began to slacken. Then, as they rode across the town limits, it petered out altogether. This enabled them to observe the county seat rather more clearly than they would otherwise have done.

Elk City was yet another cattle town, like Horseshoe Bend, although somewhat larger. Its main street was longer than that of Horseshoe Bend, and it boasted three saloons to the other's two. Also, whereas Horseshoe Bend had only a couple of streets leading off Main Street, Elk City had several.

It was on the corner of Main Street and East Street that Jack Stone and his companions found the law office. They dismounted and tied their horses to the hitching-rail outside. Then they clambered up the short flight of wooden steps to the stoop. And, led by Stone, they plunged into the office.

The law office consisted of one large rectangular-shaped room, with a door at its far end leading off to the cells situated in its rear quarters. A black pot-bellied stove exuded some heat in its immediate vicinity, but did not adequately heat the office. Consequently, the man sitting behind the room's one desk remained swathed in a bulky buckskin coat. His badge of office was presumably attached to either his shirt or his jacket since it was hidden from view beneath the coat. On his head he wore a low-crowned, wide-brimmed black Stetson.

Sheriff Beau Flanders was a lanky, thin-faced fellow in his late thirties. He had dark hair, a pair of disconcertingly penetrating blue eyes, an aquiline nose, wide mouth and lantern jaw. He had been county sheriff for the best part of a decade and, with the help of his deputies, had kept law and order pretty well in Moose County. At present, these deputies were out and about the county on a variety of assignments and the sheriff was in sole charge of the law office.

He looked up as Stone and the others entered, and slowly removed the cigar from his mouth.

'Howdy,' he said. 'Can I help you folks?'

'Yes, Sheriff, you sure can,' said Stone, 'but it's a long story.'

'OK,' said Flanders. 'Grab yourselves some chairs, sit down an' say what you've gotta say.'

They promptly did as they were bid and, when they had grouped themselves in front of the desk, Stone began.

'There's trouble brewin' in Horseshoe Bend. 'Deed, it has been for some time,' he said.

'Is that so?' drawled Flanders.

'It is.'

'Wa'al, cain't Marshal Murray handle it?'

'I don't think so.'

'He ain't wired for help.'

'No.'

'Then . . . ?'

'You'd best read this,' said Redford, handing the sheriff the Reverend Daniel Dunwoody's letter.

Flanders took the letter, opened it slowly and began to read. Dunwoody had given a full account of matters in Horseshoe Bend from the arrival of Leroy Cheney in the spring up until the present time and, consequently, the letter took some time to read. Eventually, though, Flanders finished reading and laid the pastor's letter down on the desk in front of him. He once again removed the cigar from his mouth and addressed his visitors.

'The Reverend Dunwoody seems to want me to take some of my deppities, ride over to Horseshoe Bend an' run Mr Leroy Cheney an' his pals outa town,' he remarked.

'That's the general idea,' agreed Stone.

'Cain't be done.'

'Whaddya mean?' growled the Kentuckian.

'I mean, I cain't act on hearsay, not without Marshal Murray's say-so. He *is* the law in Horseshore Bend, after all.'

'Are you sayin' you don't b'lieve the Reverend?' demanded Coyote Kate.

'No, I ain't sayin' that,' replied Flanders.

'Then, what are you sayin'?' enquired Pete Redford.

'The Reverend is reportin' what he's been told. Right?'

'Yes,' said Kate.

'But he has not himself been coerced into payin' Mr Cheney tribute?'

'No,' said Stone.

'Then, what is contained in his letter

is simply hearsay.'

'Even so . . . '

'Why hasn't Marshal Murray intervened?'

'Because he cain't hope to take on Jake Inglis an' his gang an' win.'

'Then why hasn't he wired me for help?'

'Mebbe 'cause Leroy Cheney threatened to harm his family if'n he did.'

'Mebbe ain't good enough.' Flanders eyed the three in turn. 'None of you is payin' tribute to Cheney, are you?'

'No, me an' Pete here, we're jest passin' through, though I am an ol' pal of the Reverend. But Kate's from Horseshoe Bend, an' she has had her hosses run off by Inglis an' his gun-totin' buddies.'

'Yeah, that was mentioned in the letter, though it's somethin' they deny.'

'So?'

'So, what I need is real evidence 'gainst Cheney an' his associates.'

'What kinda evidence?'

'A written complaint would do. But it would have to be written by someone who is actually bein' forced to pay tribute to Cheney. 'Deed, you furnish me with six such affidavits an' I'll be glad to intervene. That's the best I can offer.'

'Six?'

'That's what I said.'

Stone and his companions exchanged glances. Sheriff Beau Flanders was evidently the kind of peace officer who liked to play everything by the book. He wanted abundant proof that Marshal Bill Murray was failing to maintain law and order properly before he would invade the town over which Murray had jurisdiction.

'OK,' said Stone, 'we'll git you your affidavits.'

'You do that, folks, an' I'll act,' stated Flanders.

'Thank you, Sheriff.'

The three rose and left the sheriff to his paperwork and his cigar.

'You didn't tell the sheriff 'bout how we was ambushed,' said Redford, once they were outside on the stoop and out of earshot.

'Wa'al, I didn't know how he'd react. An' I daren't risk his holdin' us while he investigates the killin's,' replied the Kentuckian.

'No, we needs head straight back to Horseshoe Bend an' persuade folks to write out them complaints,' said Kate.

'You think we can git those six affidavits?' enquired Redford.

'We'll git 'em. We gotta,' said Coyote Kate grimly.

'Folks could be scared to sign 'em,' pointed out the Texan.

'They'll sign 'em, even if I have to hold my shotgun to their heads!' retorted Kate.

Stone grinned.

'Yeah. Wa'al, before we head back an' hold a shotgun to anyone's head, I figure we'd best git ourselves somethin' to eat,' he said.

His two young companions nodded their agreement. The ride through the snowstorm had given them all a healthy appetite.

And so it was that they adjourned to

Aunt Betsy's Eating-house, where they lunched on pork and beans, cornbread and coffee, before setting out on the return journey. This time, though, they did not have the falling snow to contend with. A cold wind blew, but overhead the sky was azure-blue and the sun shone.

# 5

It was almost noon and there were few customers in the Black Stallion saloon. The four remaining members of Jake Inglis's gang were sitting at one of the tables playing poker, and half a dozen drinkers lounged against the bar. They were being served by a single bartender, since the other employed by Leroy Cheney was due, like Cheney's sporting women, to come on duty much later in the day. As for the saloon-keeper, he was closeted in his private office with his cousin. A bottle of Cheney's best rye whiskey stood on the desk between them, and both men were drinking and smoking large cigars. Neither man looked particularly happy.

Leroy Cheney removed the fob-watch from the pocket of his green velvet vest and studied it closely.

'Hal an' Nat should've been back in

town by now,' he commented.

His bear-like cousin shifted uneasily in his chair and downed a large slug of whiskey. Then he carefully refilled his glass.

'I reckon them two strangers *did* take the fork to Elk City,' he rasped.

'So do I,' said Cheney.

'Wa'al, shootin' 'em wouldn't take no time, but hidin' the bodies some place where they ain't likely to be discovered could have caused Hal an' Nat to remain out there for quite a while,' said Inglis.

'Not this long, surely?'

'Hmm. I dunno.'

'Those two strangers left town 'bout breakfast time an' the fork is situated a mere four miles down the trail.'

'That there snowstorm could've held the brothers up.'

'Mebbe. But it's ceased now. So, hows about you detailin' a coupla your boys to go look for 'em?'

'Yeah. OK, I'll do that.'

Jake Inglis threw back his whiskey

and clambered to his feet. Then he left the office and strode purposefully across the bar-room to where the four shootists were playing poker. As he approached, they had just concluded a hand, Red Burton winning with a flush, consisting of a king, ten, nine, eight and four in diamonds.

'Hi, Jake. Wanta join us?' he enquired.

Inglis shook his head.

'Nope. An' I'm gonna have to break up your game,' he said.

'Whaddya mean,' growled Red Burton, who was reluctant to stop playing since he was clearly on a winning streak.

'Wa'al, it's like this,' said Inglis. 'Hal an' Nat are long overdue an' I want a coupla you boys to go look for 'em.'

'Aw, shucks, Jake, they ain't been gone that long!' exclaimed Burton.

'I ain't arguin', Red,' rasped Inglis. 'You an' Timmy git saddled up an' ride on out there.'

Timmy Tinker pulled at his whiskers and scowled. He, too, wanted to continue the game of poker, in his case in order to recoup some of his losses. Also, it was comparatively warm inside the saloon.

'There's a blizzard blowin' out there,' he protested.

'No, there ain't. It stopped some time back,' retorted Inglis. 'Now git goin' you two, 'fore I git sore,' he added ominously.

The two shootists took the hint, for Jake Inglis was not only respected, but feared by all his gang. They rose and reluctantly left the saloon.

The ride out to the spot where the trail forked was an easy one. It was no longer snowing, the wind had dropped and, although there was some fresh snow on the trail, there were no drifts.

A quarter of a mile further on, in the direction of Elk City, Red Burton and Timmy Tinker came across the two riderless horses. A little way off, half-buried in the snow, they found the corpses of the Rogers brothers. The two men dismounted and went over and inspected the bodies.

'Shot. Both of 'em,' announced Burton.

'By them two strangers, the Reverend's buddy an' the cowboy?' said Tinker.

'Who else?' growled Burton.

'Mr Cheney ain't gonna be none too pleased.'

'Neither is Jake. Come on, let's git 'em back to Horseshoe Bend.'

They heaved the corpses across their saddles and tied them on, using some cord, which Burton found in his saddle-bag. Then, with Burton leading Hal Rogers's horse, and Tinker leading Nat Rogers's, they set off back the way they had come.

Their arrival in Horseshoe Bend caused quite a stir. They halted in front of the Black Stallion saloon and a crowd quickly gathered. Foremost among those present were Marshal Bill Murray, Norman Black, Doc Shaw and the mortician, Ben Brady, while Fred Newton appeared in the doorway of the *Chronicle* office, Sam Flanagan stepped on to the stoop outside his saloon and Lettie Crichton watched from the window of her dry-goods store. As for Leroy Cheney, he, along with Jake Inglis, Roscoe Jonson and Roy Davin, hurriedly emerged from the Black Stallion.

'What in tarnation's happened?' demanded the saloon-keeper.

'Nat an' Hal, they're both dead,' replied Red Burton. 'We found 'em just past the fork to Elk City.'

'Shot,' added Timmy Tinker.

'By whom?' enquired Marshal Bill Murray.

'By bandits, no doubt,' shouted Fred Newton.

'Whaddya mean?' rasped the mar-shal.

'Wa'al, wasn't Les Dalton set upon by bandits on that stretch of trail an', as for John Martin, he too was shot dead. I guess it was the same gang, wouldn't you say, Marshal?' said Newton slyly.

While Marshal Bill Murray looked distinctly uncomfortable, Leroy Cheney glared balefully at the elderly newspaperman. The saloon-keeper did not like having the fiction he had concocted used, in this case, against him. He determined shortly to make a move to close down the *Chronicle*. Fred Newton had become, in Cheney's opinion, altogether too smart for his own good.

The marshal, meantime, muttered that he supposed it could have been bandits. He did not know what else to say. This half-hearted and inconclusive response did nothing to decrease Cheney's displeasure.

'OK,' he said, 'let's remove the bodies to the funeral parlour.'

Red Burton and Timmy Tinker led the two horses bearing Hal and Nat Rogers's corpses across the street to Ben Brady's premises. The mortician, in his tall stovepipe hat and long black coat, trotted along behind. He rubbed his hands gleefully.

The crowd prepared to disperse at this point, but were delayed by the sudden arrival of Jack Stone, Pete

Redford and Coyote Kate Driscoll. They entered from the opposite direction to that taken by Red Burton and Timmy Tinker. They had taken a chance that Coyote Kate's route through the mountains would still be passable and they had been lucky. Wolf Pass remained open.

'What the hell are they doin' back in town?' Cheney hissed in Bill Murray's ear. 'I thought you told 'em to hightail it outa here?'

'I sure did,' said Murray.

'Wa'al, what are you gonna do 'bout it?'

'I . . . er . . . um . . . '

'Challenge 'em or, by God, I'll let Jake an' the boys shoot their goddam heads off!'

'We . . . we don't want no bloodshed.' Murray gulped and then hastily addressed Stone and his companions, who had ridden up to the hitching-rail in front of Flanagan's Saloon. 'You two!' he yelled. 'I told you to leave town!'

'We did leave town,' said Stone

equably. 'But now we're back.'

'I wanted you outa town for good!'

'You didn't actually say that, Marshal,' said the Kentuckian.

'Wa'al, that is what I meant!' cried Murray.

'Guess we misunderstood you, then,' interjected Redford.

'There was no misunderstanding. They have deliberately defied you, Marshal,' said Cheney.

'We will leave for good tomorrow,' said Stone.

'I say you leave now,' stated Murray.

'It'll be dark soon. We git lost out there, we could easily die in a snowdrift. You wouldn't want that on your conscience, Marshal.'

Murray sighed, while, beside him, Leroy Cheney fumed silently.

'No,' the marshal said at last. 'OK, then, you can stay one more night. But, when you leave tomorrow, you don't come back. Is *that* understood?'

'Perfectly, Marshal.'

'Wait a minute!' cried Cheney. 'What

about Hal an' Nat?'

'Who?' asked Stone innocently.

'You know who. You . . . ' Cheney paused. He could scarcely accuse Stone of gunning them down without publicly admitting that they had been lying in wait for the Kentuckian.

At this juncture, Fred Newton chipped in.

'They are the two of Mr Cheney's associates you had a little bother with yesterday,' he explained cheerfully. 'Jest been carted off to the funeral parlour. It seems they were gunned down by bandits while on their way to Elk City.'

'Yeah,' said Stone. 'The Reverend mentioned last night that there have been a coupla incidents involvin' bandits out on the trail. Guess me an' Pete are darned lucky they didn't attack us.'

Leroy Cheney, white with rage, tapped his cousin on the shoulder.

'Come on, Jake,' he said. 'Let's go git us a drink. I need one badly.' Then he turned to the marshal and snarled, 'Bill, you better make sure those fellers do leave town tomorrow, otherwise there *will* be bloodshed. OK?'

'Yeah. Sure thing, Mr Cheney,' mumbled the marshal nervously.

As Leroy Cheney and his associates retreated into the Black Stallion and the crowd gradually began to break up, Stone and his two companions dismounted, hitched their horses to the rail and clattered up the wooden steps on to the stoop in front of Flanagan's saloon. The saloon-keeper had vanished inside, but Fred Newton remained standing outside his newspaper office.

'Well done, fellers,' he said, winking at the Kentuckian and the young Texan. 'Good riddance to bad rubbish, eh?'

'I don't know what you're talkin' about.' Stone grinned.

''Course you don't,' replied Newton jocularly, adding, 'I reckon, when it comes to buryin' them, the Reverend will have a hard job to say anythin' good about them.'

'Where is Daniel, by the way? I didn't

notice him in the crowd,' said Stone.

'He's off visitin' the sick. Old Mrs Chatterton. She lives out past Coyote's place,' replied the newspaperman.

'That's so,' said Kate.

'Ah, right!' said Stone, and he followed the other two into the saloon.

When they reached the bar, they found two whiskeys and a mug of steaming-hot coffee awaiting them. A beaming Sam Flanagan announced jovially, 'They're on the house.'

'Thanks,' said Stone.

'My pleasure. You were the ones who filled Hal an' Nat Rogers full of holes, weren't you?' remarked the saloon-keeper.

'Yeah. They tried to ambush Jack an' me. Luckily, Kate intervened an' then Jack shot 'em,' said Redford.

'So, you fellers got through to Elk City?'

'We sure did.'

'An' you delivered the Reverend's letter to Sheriff Beau Flanders?'

'Yup.'

'But he ain't prepared to act upon it,' said Stone.

'He ain't?'

'Nope. Reckons, since Daniel ain't payin' tribute to Leroy Cheney, it's no more'n hearsay.'

'Wa'al, where does that leave us?' demanded Flanagan, his big, beaming smile slowly fading.

'The sheriff is prepared to act,' said Kate. 'But only if'n we provide him with affidavits signed by no fewer than six folks who have been coerced into payin' Cheney protection money.'

'OK. In that case, I figure we'd best draft us that affidavit,' stated Flanagan.

While the others supped their drinks, he vanished into the saloon's rear quarters. A couple of minutes later, he reappeared clutching a sheaf of papers, a quill pen and a bottle of black ink.

'Now,' he said, 'what are we gonna put?'

'Give me one of them sheets of paper an' I'll see what I can do,' proffered Kate.

Flanagan handed the girl a sheet of paper. She took up the pen, dipped it into the bottle of ink and began to write. The draft she came up with was marred by several crossings out, but it finally read as follows:

*I hereby swear that I have been forced to pay a regular tribute to Leroy Cheney. This is gathered each week by Cheney's cousin, Jake Inglis, or by one of his associates, and is made under threat of violence.*

'We git the six to make this complaint, addin' to it if they want,' said Kate. 'I mean, Sid Harrison was beaten up 'fore he agreed to pay. He might like to put that in his affidavit.'

'Good thinkin', Coyote,' said Flanagan.

'This draft OK with you fellers?' Kate asked of Stone and Redford.

'Yeah,' said Stone.

'It reads jest fine,' commented the young Texan.

'Good! Then let me write out six

copies, to take round to the folks who are gonna make the complaints,' said Kate.

This she proceeded to do, taking her time so that she made no mistakes. When she had finished, the six affidavits were laid on the mahogany counter-top to dry.

'Now, all we gotta do is decide who we intend to approach,' said Flanagan. 'Wa'al, since Pete an' me don't know the local citizens, I guess it's up to you an' Kate to choose,' said Stone. 'When you have done that, we'll do the visitin'.'

'You had best leave them visits until after dark, for you don't want Cheney an' his gang to git wind of what we're up to,' said the girl.

'No.'

Kate turned to the saloon-keeper.

'Who d'you think we should ask, Sam?'

The saloon-keeper scratched his head. This was not going to be easy, for he reckoned that most of Horseshoe

Bend's citizens would be too scared to testify against Leroy Cheney and his gang.

'Hows about you, Coyote?' he growled.

The girl shook her head.

'No, Sam,' she said. 'I ain't payin' no tribute.'

'But that business with your hosses . . .'

'I cain't prove nuthin'. It's my word agin' Jake Inglis's an', remember, every danged one of them no-account critters, who attacked my ranch an' drove off my hosses, was masked.'

'So, who do you suggest?'

'Wa'al, there's you, of course, Sam.'

'I could, but it'd be better to git other folks to sign, folks who ain't in direct competition with Leroy Cheney. The sheriff might consider me to be a hostile witness.'

'Hmm. That's a point.'

'So, whaddya think, Coyote?'

'Norman Black was pretty sore 'bout bein' displaced as mayor. I figure he'd be prepared to sign one of them affidavits.' Kate turned to her two companions. 'He's the proprietor of the Horseshoe Bend Hotel. You're sure to find him there,' she said.

'OK,' said Stone. 'An' next?'

'Hows about Ben Brady,' suggested Flanagan. 'He has always struck me as bein' a pretty cool customer.'

'Yeah, I agree,' said Kate. Again she turned to Stone and Redford. 'He's the town's mortician an' lives above his funeral parlour,' she explained.

'What about that feller outside the newspaper office?' enquired Pete Redford. 'He seemed kinda spunky.'

'Fred Newton. He has quarters behind that office. You could do worse than to drop in on him,' agreed Sam Flanagan.

'Three down an' three to go,' said Stone. 'If'n you're sure 'bout them first three?'

'We are,' declared Kate, while the saloon-keeper nodded his agreement.

'OK. Who's number four?' asked Redford.

'I suggest Lettie Crichton,' said Kate.

'I dunno 'bout includin' a woman in this?' remarked the Texan doubtfully.

'Why not? I'm sure she'll sign. I tell you, Lettie's madder'n a grizzly in a trap! She told me it was only when Jake Inglis made some sly comment, 'bout what a pity it'd be if'n her dry-goods store went up in flames, that she agreed to pay. After all, he wasn't jest threatenin' her business, he was also threatenin' her home.'

'She lives on the premises, then?' said Redford.

'Yup, she does.'

'OK.'

'We spoke earlier 'bout Sid Harrison gittin' beaten up,' interjected Flanagan. 'Mebbe we could enlist him? As Coyote remarked, he might wanta mention that at the end of his affidavit.'

'He might. Or he might be too darned scared to git involved,' said Stone.

'Let's at least try him,' said Kate.

'If you think so. That leaves us with jest one more to find,' commented Stone.

Kate and the saloon-keeper thought for a few moments. Then Sam Flanagan spoke up.

'So far, we've chosen folks who live in Horseshoe Bend. How's about we choose, for our sixth complainant, someone who lives outside the town?'

'Yeah,' said Kate. 'That's a good idea, for I know all the homesteaders are payin' Leroy Cheney protection money. An' those I've spoken to are pretty sore about it.'

'Which of 'em d'you reckon we should approach?' enquired Flanagan.

'My next-door neighbour, Ollie Prout, is a mean sonofabitch. I don't like the feller, but he's sure to be really riled up. Partin' with money is somethin' he hates doin',' said Kate.

'OK, let's make him our sixth complainant,' said Flanagan. He smiled at Stone and the young Texan. 'You fellers happy with those we've listed?'

'Yeah, though what if one or more of 'em refuses to sign the affidavit?' growled Stone.

'That ain't likely,' said Kate.

'But it's possible.'

'Yes, it's possible, I guess.' The girl frowned and said, 'You'll jest have to bind anyone who refuses to silence, an' then find a replacement. The Reverend will come up with someone, or you can mosey along here an' ask Sam.'

'That's right,' agreed the saloon-keeper.

'Don't worry. One way or another, we'll git our six affidavits,' stated Kate confidently.

The Kentuckian and the Texan both grinned. They liked the seventeen-year-old's optimism and her determination.

'OK,' said Stone. 'Let's drink up an' git goin'. Pete an' me, we'll report back to Daniel an' then, as soon as it's dark, we'll slip out an' git them affidavits signed.'

'Make sure that none of Cheney's gang sees you,' warned Kate.

'We'll be careful,' said Stone.

With that, he and Redford threw back the remains of their whiskeys,

Kate finished her coffee and, having picked up the affidavits, the three of them took their leave of Sam Flanagan.

A few minutes later, the two men were cantering along Main Street. towards the Reverend Daniel Dunwoody's home on the edge of town, while Coyote Kate was riding her grey mare in the opposite direction, out to her now horseless horse ranch. Leroy Cheney watched them go. Then he turned and retreated across the barroom of the Black Stallion saloon to where his cousin stood drinking at the bar-counter.

'Wa'al?' said Jake Inglis.

'I dunno,' said Cheney. 'I've got a nasty feelin' about the Reverend's buddy an' that cowboy.'

'Mebbe me an' the boys should go an' . . . ?'

'No, not yet, Jake. I don't wanta stir things up. If'n them two fellers leave town tomorrow an' don't come back, I figure that's for the best. We sure as hell don't wanta give Sheriff Beau Flanders an excuse to come here an' launch an investigation.'

'I guess not,' said Inglis.

'Definitely not,' said Cheney. 'I reckon that somehow or other the pair spotted Hal an' Nat lyin' in wait for 'em an' then proceeded to out-gun the brothers.'

'So?'

'So, they must've been headed for Elk City. Which means that they spoke to the sheriff; but failed to persuade him to take any action. Otherwise he'd be here now.' Cheney grinned. 'I figure they only returned to Horseshoe Bend so as to let the Reverend know he could expect no help from Sheriff Flanders.'

'Hmm. That makes sense, Leroy.'

'Therefore, mebbe this time they really will head south,' concluded the saloon-keeper.

# 6

Following his call upon the ailing Mrs Chatterton, the Reverend Daniel Dunwoody arrived home to find Jack Stone and Pete Redford enjoying coffee and cookies with Hannah, while the children played upstairs.

Stone informed his friend of the day's happenings and of their plan to provide Sheriff Beau Flanders with half a dozen affidavits.

'Well, Jack, it's certainly been quite a day!' declared Dunwoody.

'An' it ain't over yet,' said Stone.

'No. But let us hope there will be no further killings.'

'There needn't be. Pete an' me, we'll jest git them affidavits signed, an' then tomorrow we'll take 'em over to Elk City an' hand 'em in to Sheriff Flanders.' Stone smiled wryly and added, 'He can handle things from there on.'

'Yes.'

'We're gonna each approach three folks,' explained Pete Redford. 'Jack is to call on Sid Harrison, Lettie Crichton an' Ollie Prout, while I visit Norman Black, Fred Newton an' Ben Brady.'

'We know where to find five of 'em, but you'll need to give me instructions 'bout how to git to Ollie Prout's homestead,' added Stone.

The pastor nodded.

'You can't miss his place. It's the first homestead you come across on the far side of town. Pass it an' you reach Kate Driscoll's one-time horse ranch. I guess it's a couple of miles at most beyond the town limits.'

'Thanks, Daniel. That sounds easy enough to find.' Stone glanced out of the window and promptly finished drinking his coffee. 'It's dark outside. I reckon, Pete, that you an' me better git goin',' he said.

'I'll hold back supper till you return,' remarked Hannah, with a smile.

'We'll look forward to that,' said Stone.

He and Pete Redford stepped out into the darkness. There were lights on in some of the stores and houses along Main Street, but only Dunwoody's house was lit up at that end of Horseshoe Bend. Opposite, the church stood black and silent, its steeple stark against the evening sky.

'I figure we should avoid Main Street an' approach everybody from the rear,' said the Kentuckian.

'Good idea, Jack. I guess I'll circle round behind the Reverend's house, since the places I intend visitin' are on this side of Main Street,' said Redford.

'Yeah. Wa'al, apart from Ollie Prout, my folks live across the street. So, I'll see you back here later,' replied Stone.

Pete Redford watched the Kentuckian unhitch his bay gelding, lead it across the street and out on to the snowbound plain. Soon Stone disappeared into the gathering darkness and Redford turned and trudged off through the snow, skirting Dunwoody's house and then proceeding past the back of the premises lining the western side of Main Street.

Although the light of the stars prevented the evening from being pitch-black, nevertheless it remained pretty dark and consequently, Pete Redford, a stranger in town, found it quite difficult to distinguish the various buildings as he made his way slowly past their rear quarters.

However, his intended first port of call was the Horseshoe Bend Hotel and, since this was easily the largest building in town and also one of the few to boast two storeys, Redford confidently left the edge of the plain and approached it. Ahead of him lay a small yard, containing a wagon, several empty beer-barrels and a number of crates holding empty whiskey-bottles. He cautiously wended his way between these barrels and crates until, eventually, he reached the hotel's back door. He tried the doorhandle. It turned and he let himself in.

Redford found himself in a large storeroom. Here, too, were beer-barrels and crates of whiskey-bottles, but these were all full. His problem now was to find Norman Black without, at the same time, someone seeing him. By sheer good fortune, this problem was solved for, at that very moment, Norman Black entered the storeroom. He had come to fetch some bottles of whiskey with which to replenish his stock behind the hotel bar.

Norman Black was a tall, silver-haired man, with fine, handsome features and a large walrus moustache. He wore a black Prince Albert coat, a snow-white shirt with ruffled collar, a bootlace tie, black velvet vest and black trousers, and highly polished black shoes. He normally cut a most distinguished figure, but his shock at so unexpectedly encountering the young Texan caused him to lose his usual dignified air.

'Wh . . . what are . . . are you doin'

here?' he exclaimed in alarm.

'It's OK. I ain't come to rob you, if that's what you're thinkin',' said Redford.

'Then what have you come to do?' demanded the hotelier.

'I wanted a quiet word with you.'

'Most folks who want to speak to me enter the premises through the front door.'

'You don't understand. I didn't want nobody to see me talkin' to you.'

Norman Black's look changed from one of alarm to one of puzzlement.

'You had better explain,' he said curiously. Then, all at once, he recognized the Texan. 'You're one of those two fellers who rode into town yesterday,' he stated.

'That's right.'

'Your buddy knocked the livin' daylights outa the Rogers brothers.' Norman Black paused and gasped, 'You an' he wouldn't have had anythin' to do with them gittin' shot out on the trail, would you?'

Pete Redford grinned.

'You surely don't expect me to answer that, Mr Black?' he said quietly.

'No.'

'Good, 'cause I ain't gonna. Now, as to why I'm here, I need your help.'

'To do what?'

'Rid this town of Leroy Cheney an' his pals for good.'

'I . . . I ain't no hand with a gun. If you're lookin' for folks to stand up an' fight 'em . . . '

'No. All I want you to do is sign this here affidavit.'

So saying, Redford handed the hotelier one of the six affidavits composed by Coyote Kate. Norman Black carefully read it, not once, but three times. The colour faded from his cheeks as he studied the words and, when he looked up, there was fear in his eyes.

'You . . . you want me to s-sign this?' he exclaimed, tapping the sheet of paper with a trembling finger.

'Yup. That's the idea,' said Redford.

'It'd be like signing my own death warrant.'

'Leroy Cheney ain't gonna know you've signed it. I guarantee that.'

'Who . . . who would know?'

'Why jest the Reverend an' me an' my buddy, Jack Stone. You sign that there affidavit an' I'll deliver it to Sheriff Beau Flanders in Elk City. Then — '

'So, he'll know!'

'Sure, he'll know. That's what he needs to enable him to act agin' Cheney. He won't act on hearsay. He wants a complaint signed by someone who Cheney's actually threatened.'

'I ain't the only person he's threatened!'

'No, that's true.'

'The whole goddam town is payin' him tribute.'

'Yup.'

'So, why pick on me? Why should I be the one who makes the complaint?'

'Wa'al, why not you?' enquired Redford evenly. 'After all, you was once mayor of Horseshoe Bend. The sheriff sure as hell couldn't ignore a complaint made by such a prominent citizen as yourself.'

The young Texan had reckoned that perhaps a little flattery might persuade Norman Black to co-operate. And in this he was right. The hotelier still regarded himself as the rightful holder of the office of mayor. As a result, he probably hated Leroy Cheney more than most. Yes, he told himself, he was indeed the very man to persuade Sheriff Flanders to act.

'Very well,' he said at last. 'I'll sign. But you be sure not to let Cheney git wind of it.'

'Don't worry, Mr Black, he won't know nuthin' till Sheriff Flanders an' his deppities ride into town to arrest him,' said Redford reassuringly. ''Sides, you ain't gonna be the only one to sign an affidavit like this here.'

'No?'

'No, sirree! Me an' Jack Stone are collectin' several other affidavits to hand to Sheriff Flanders. Presented with that much evidence, he will jest have to take action agin' Cheney an' his cousin.'

'I guess so, but who are the other complainants?'

'I cain't tell you that, Mr Black, any more'n I can tell them that you're one of 'em.'

Norman Black smiled and nodded.

'Yeah. That's good. There ain't no need for any of us to know who the others are.'

'Exactly.'

'OK, I'll take the affidavit through to my office to sign. You wait here.'

Norman Black was gone for only a few minutes. Then he returned and handed Pete Redford the signed affidavit.

'Thanks, Mr Black. You won't regret this,' said the Texan.

'I sure as hell hope not,' replied the hotelier.

Redford smiled and quietly left by the hotel's back door. He recalled that the funeral parlour was situated next but one to Black's establishment. And so it proved. In response to his knocking, the lugubrious-looking Ben Brady opened the rear door, clad in his long black coat, but minus the stovepipe hat. The mortician glared suspiciously at his unexpected visitor.

'Whaddya want?' he enquired sharply.

'I want what I b'lieve you want: the downfall of Leroy Cheney an' his bunch of no-account gunslingers.'

'Hmm. You'd best step inside.'

Ben Brady led his caller upstairs and into a small, cosy sitting room, and indicated that he should sit down. Then, when both men were settled in the mortician's easy-chairs, he growled, 'An' jest how are you proposin' to achieve this?'

'Sheriff Beau Flanders has promised to act agin' Cheney, but only if he is provided with written complaints by those whom Cheney is blackmailin'.'

'Complaints?'

'Yeah. He figures one ain't enough. He needs several, an' I was hopin' you'd be prepared to sign one of 'em.' Redford handed the mortician the second of his three affidavits. 'Whaddya say?' he asked anxiously.

Brady scratched his head, then removed and polished his spectacles. Like the hotelier before him, he was less than enthusiastic. He replaced the spectacles and studied the affidavit for some minutes. At last he raised his eyes, looked the young Texan straight in the eye and sighed deeply.

'OK,' he said. 'I'll sign.'

'Thank you,' said Redford.

The Texan's next port of call was the office of the Horseshoe Bend *Chronicle*. Before leaving the funeral parlour, he enquired of Ben Brady how many doors further down the street it lay. By so doing, he realized that he was revealing the identity of a potential signatory to the mortician. But he felt he had no choice in the matter. He needed Brady's direction to enable him to distinguish the rear of Fred Newton's premises from the others on that side of Main Street.

Newton, although also surprised by Redford's visit, was rather more welcoming than either the hotelier or the mortician had been.

'Come in! Come in!' he cried.

Redford needed no second bidding. He was only too happy to leave the edge of the snowbound plain and escape from the cold night air.

Fred Newton had a small, neat parlour, similar in size to Ben Brady's sitting room. It was equally warm and cosy and no sooner were he and his visitor ensconced in a couple of well-worn leather armchairs, on either side of the elderly newspaperman's roaring fire, than Pete Redford explained the reason for his visit.

He handed Newton the third of his affidavits and awaited the other's response.

'So, Beau Flanders has agreed to intervene,' said Newton approvingly. ''Bout time, for Bill Murray sure ain't up to the job.'

'Yes, wa'al, the marshal is kinda outnumbered.'

'He has a deppity.'

'Even so, he wouldn't stand a chance agin' that gang of desperadoes.'

'Nope, guess not. Cheney an' his ruffianly cousin have got this town pretty well under their thumbs.'

'But not for much longer, Mr Newton,' said Redford. 'When me an' Jack Stone present the sheriff with our affidavits, he'll be forced to take action.'

'I'll jest sign this one, then,' said the newspaper-man eagerly.

Pete Redford grinned. He had at last come upon someone who was actually anxious to make a complaint against Leroy Cheney.

While the young Texan was getting his three affidavits signed, Jack Stone was similarly occupied on the opposite side of Main Street. He had to delay his first call, however, for, as he approached the rear of Lettie Crichton's dry-goods store, he observed through her lighted window that she already had a visitor.

Inside her parlour Lettie stood glaring belligerently at the bearded giant, Roy Davin. Small and sturdy in her neat grey gown, her rosy-red cheeks flaming and her bright blue eyes sparkling with anger, Lettie was giving the shootist a piece of her mind. She might be grey-haired, in her sixties and a good foot shorter than he, yet she was determined not to be intimidated by Leroy Cheney's huge enforcer.

'I'll pay you what you demand, you brute,' she snapped. 'But you can tell that stinkin', no-good skunk, Cheney, that extortin' money from a helpless widow-woman is the work of a snivellin' coward.'

Roy Davin stared back at the little shopkeeper, his features expressing both anger and embarrassment. He looked and felt distinctly uncomfortable.

'Jest pay up an' shuddup!' he rasped.

'Don't tell me to shut up in my own home,' retorted Lettie, as she counted out the tribute demanded of her. And, upon placing the last coin in Davin's huge hand, she said peremptorily, 'Now git outa my house!'

Davin looked as though he was about to strike the widow, but changed his mind, turned abruptly on his heel and stomped off, slamming the parlour door shut behind him.

Jack Stone waited for a few moments, to give the gunslinger time to walk through Lettie Crichton's shop and out into Main Street. Then he tapped on the windowpane. Lettie glanced towards the window and peered out into the darkness outside. Stone moved along and tapped again, this time on the rear door of the premises.

Lettie opened the door and stared at the Kentuckian.

'You're one of them two fellers who rode into town yesterday afternoon,' she said.

'That's right, ma'am. Stone's the name. Jack Stone,' he replied.

'Wa'al, you've sure stirred things up since then, Mr Stone.'

'An' I'm proposin' to stir 'em up some more.'

'Come in, then, an' tell me all about it.'

Stone let go of the gelding's bridle. He patted the gelding gently, then followed Lettie inside, where he explained what was needed.

'You got others prepared to sign these affidavits?' asked Lettie.

'Yup. I reckon we'll present the sheriff with enough signatories to satisfy him,' said Stone.

'I hope you are right, Mr Stone.'

'You'll sign?'

'I surely will.'

When the widow had signed the complaint and handed it back to him, the Kentuckian thanked her and said, 'I'll be moseyin' along, for I've still got another coupla signatures to collect.'

'Good luck, then.'

'Thanks.'

Stone recalled that Sid Harrison's general store was three premises further on down Main Street. Therefore, leading the gelding by its bridle, he left the widow's dry-goods store and tramped through the snow towards his second objective.

He cautiously approached the rear window of the general store and peered in. Neither Roy Davin nor any other of Leroy Cheney's enforcers was visiting the storekeeper. Sid Harrison sat at his kitchen table, in front of a roaring fire, happily consuming his supper. He had just swallowed the last mouthful when Stone tapped loudly on his back door.

The storekeeper was a small, scrawny fellow in his late fifties, with a shock of snow-white hair, a large, drooping moustache of the same hue and a pair of faded blue eyes. He had removed the apron, which he wore when serving in the store, and was clad in a check shirt and well-worn denim trousers. He opened the door the merest crack and peered nervously at the big Kentuckian.

'Oh . . . oh . . . you're the Reverend's buddy, ain't you?' he murmured.

'That's right, Mr Harrison. Jack Stone's the name.'

'Wa'al, er, you'd best come in outa the cold.'

'Thank you.'

'So, what can I do for you?' enquired Harrison, once they were both seated on either side of his kitchen fire.

'I want you to sign an affidavit,' replied Stone, and he proceeded to inform the storekeeper of the plan to force Sheriff Beau Flanders to take action against Leroy Cheney and his gang. He concluded by handing Harrison one of the affidavits and saying, 'You can, if you like, add an account of the beatin' dished out to you by them no-account critters.'

Sid Harrison scowled at the memory of it. A broken nose, two black eyes, three cracked ribs and sundry bruises had laid him up for several days. A widower, he had had to rely upon his married daughter to come over and manage the store until he eventually recovered.

'The bastards threatened to kill me if'n I refused to pay a second time,' he growled.

'So, you'll sign?' said Stone.

'You betcha I'll sign,' he replied, with a gleam in his eye. 'I want Leroy an' his cousin to swing. You know they, or rather their henchmen, murdered John Martin, our local dentist, out on the trail?'

'It couldn't be proved, though.'

'No.' Sid Harrison carefully studied the affidavit and, after a few moments' thought, added a brief description of his beating to the text supplied by Coyote Kate. 'There you are,' he said. 'That should do the trick.'

Stone read the storekeeper's words and nodded.

'That's jest fine,' he said.

'Wa'al, you take care Cheney's shootists don't bushwhack you along the trail,' said Harrison gravely.

'I shall, though, since we failed to enlist Sheriff Flanders' aid earlier, I figure they won't expect us to try a second time.'

'Mebbe not.'

'Anyway, I'll be goin'. I got me one

more signatory to visit.'

'Good luck, then, Mr Stone.'

'Thanks.'

The Kentuckian slipped out of the store's back door and swiftly mounted the gelding. He skirted the town and only joined the trail once he was beyond its limits. Then he set off at a canter in the direction of Ollie Prout's homestead.

A bright, starlit sky lighted his way and, with the snow along the trail hard-packed, the gelding soon covered the two miles. Shafts of yellow light spilled out from the windows of Ollie Prout's cabin. Stone smiled and turned the horse's head towards it. He pulled up in front of its covered porch, dismounted and hitched the gelding to the rail outside. Then he climbed up on to the porch and knocked upon Ollie Prout's door.

The homesteader was a tall, lean man, with thinning black hair, a pair of cold grey eyes and a long, bony face, which wore a permanent scowl. Stone could understand why Coyote Kate had said she didn't like the man.

'Mr Prout,' he said, 'let me introduce myself. Jack Stone at your — '

'I know who you are,' Prout interrupted him. 'You're that buddy of the Reverend.'

'You've heard what's been happenin' since I got here?'

'Sure have. News travels fast in an' around Horseshoe Bend.' Prout permitted himself a wintry smile. 'You ain't exactly endeared yourself to Mr Leroy Cheney, have you?' he rasped.

'Nope.'

'So whaddya want with me, Mr Stone?'

'Invite me in an' I'll explain.'

'OK. Step inside.'

The cabin consisted of three rooms: two small bedchambers and a large, rectangular-shaped room, which was kitchen and living-quarters combined. This large room was sparsely furnished and the fire a poor affair, which did little to dispel the chill in the air. Stone smiled grimly, recalling that Kate had described Prout as 'a mean sonofabitch'. He determined to get the affidavit signed and return to the warmth of the Reverend Dunwoody's home as soon as possible.

'Wa'al, Mr Prout, it's like this,' he said, and then he went on to explain his mission. He finished by saying, 'When Sheriff Flanders arrests Leroy Cheney, as he surely will, that'll be the end of you payin' the bastard tribute.'

Ollie Prout's eyes lit up. Paying a proportion of his hard-earned money to the saloon-keeper had grieved him greatly. He took hold of the affidavit, which Stone was offering him.

'I ain't the only person to be signin' one of these, am I?' he asked anxiously.

'No, there are others,' replied the Kentuckian.

'How many?'

'We're aimin' to collect six signatures.'

'Includin' mine?'

'Yup. Six altogether.'

Prout laughed harshly and remarked, 'That should be enough to satisfy the sheriff.'

'Yeah, I reckon so.'

Stone waited while the homesteader signed the complaint against Leroy Cheney and then straight away took his leave of him. With the three affidavits lodged securely inside the pocket of his buckskin jacket, Stone unhitched the gelding, mounted and set off, this time at a gallop, towards the pastor's home.

Again, rather than ride through Main Street, he skirted the town and approached the town from the far end. Consequently, when eventually he entered Dunwoody's home, having firstly stabled, fed and watered his horse, he was pretty sure that Cheney and his gang were quite unaware that he had ever left.

While Hannah busied herself preparing their supper, her husband and his two guests studied the six affidavits that Stone and Redford had obtained between them.

'So,' said Dunwoody, 'nobody refused to sign.'

'Nope, though some were keener to sign than others,' said Stone.

'That's true,' agreed Redford, with a smile.

'Anyway, we set out at first light to deliver 'em to Sheriff Flanders,' declared Stone.

'Be careful. Cheney might plan another ambush along the trail to Elk City.'

'Jest in case he does, I propose we avoid the main trail an' head there by way of Wolf Pass,' said the Kentuckian.

'Ah, yes, Coyote Kate's route!' grinned Redford.

'If it's still open,' said Dunwoody.

'It was when we returned to town earlier,' stated Stone.

'So, unless there's another snowfall between now and dawn . . . '

'Pray there won't be one, Reverend,' said Redford.

'That's right, Daniel, have a word

with Him upstairs,' said Stone, with a smile.

The Reverend Daniel Dunwoody also smiled.

'I shall certainly do that, Jack,' he murmured.

# 7

At the same time that the Reverend Daniel Dunwoody, Jack Stone and Pete Redford were discussing how they would take the affidavits to Elk City, Ollie Prout was riding his pinto into town.

The homesteader had reviewed his situation and come to the conclusion that, with some capital behind him, he could do much better than simply scratch a living from his farm. Instead of toiling away to grow and pick his own vegetables, he could perhaps open a grocery shop in, say, 'Frisco or Chicago and sell the produce of other folks' labours. Or he could branch out into a new line of business altogether. And Jack Stone had unwittingly provided him with an opportunity to raise that necessary capital. Which was why Prout was riding down Horseshoe

Bend's Main Street and heading for the Black Stallion saloon.

The bar-room was not quite as packed as it would have been on a Saturday night when the cowhands from the Lazy S, the Bar J and the High Butte ranches were in town. Nevertheless, it was doing brisk business. The bar-counter was crowded, there were two games of blackjack and one of poker in progress, the roulette table had gamblers jostling to place their bets, and Leroy Cheney's sporting women were all occupied upstairs, satisfying their clients' needs.

It was into this mêlée that Ollie Prout marched, having hitched his horse to the rail outside, stepped up on to the stoop and pushed in through the batwing doors. He paused and looked about him. He observed that the four surviving members of Jake Inglis's gang were sitting round one of the two blackjack tables, while Inglis stood up at the bar drinking beer. Of Leroy Cheney there was no sign. Ollie Prout made his way through the throng to the bar-counter, where he squeezed in beside the huge, bear-like gunslinger.

' 'Evenin', Mr Inglis,' he said, touching the brim of his black, low-brimmed Stetson and smiling obsequiously up at the shootist.

' 'Evenin', Prout,' growled Jake Inglis.

Ollie Prout chose to ignore the fact that the other had deliberately chosen not to address him as 'Mister', and he continued to smile his ingratiating smile.

'You're doin' good business,' he commented.

'We usually do,' retorted Inglis.

'I don't see Mr Cheney. Is he . . . ?'

'My cousin's busy in his office.'

'Wa'al, would it be OK if I moseyed on over there an' had a few words with him?'

'I said he was busy.'

'He'll wanta hear what I've got to say.'

Jake Inglis viewed the homesteader with an appraising eye, then growled,

'So, what have you got to say?'

'I wanta tell it to Mr Cheney.'

'Now, look here . . . '

'Why don't we both go to his office?'

Jake Inglis was tempted to shake whatever it was Ollie Prout had to say out of him. But, in the end, he relented.

'OK, let's go,' he said gruffly.

He threw back the remains of his beer, grabbed Prout by the arm and barged through the drinkers towards a door situated halfway between the bar and the small stage that stood at the opposite end of the bar-room. He tapped on the door three times.

'That you, Jake?' asked a voice from inside the office.

'Yes, Leroy, it is,' he replied.

'Then come on in.'

Inglis marched Ollie Prout into the office, slammed the door shut and announced, 'Prout here says he's got somethin' to say that you'll wanta hear.'

Leroy Cheney leant back in his chair and puffed nonchalantly on his cigar. He stared across his desk at his unexpected visitor.

'OK, Mr Prout,' he murmured politely, 'say what you have to say.'

'I have important information, which I'm prepared to divulge to you for a price.'

'For a price?' Cheney's expression hardened.

'Yes.'

'How much?'

'One thousand dollars.'

Cheney laughed, while Inglis tightened his grip on the homesteader's arm.

'Want me to beat the information outa him, Leroy?' he asked.

Cheney shook his head.

'Not yet. Only if we cain't negotiate.' He stared hard at Ollie Prout. 'Can we negotiate?' he asked softly.

Ollie Prout nodded. He had not expected Cheney to pay up without a quibble. His suggestion of $1,000 had simply been his starting gambit. He had expected to have to come down in price.

'That feller, Jack Stone, he called on me this evenin',' he said. 'Y'see, he's got a plan to rid Horseshoe Bend of you an' your associates once an' for all.'

'A viable plan?'

'Yes, indeed! You gonna pay me to tell you what it is?' Prout glanced over his shoulder at Jake Inglis and continued, 'Your cousin could beat the hell outa me, but how'd you know that what I blurted out was the truth?'

Cheney considered the matter for a moment or two.

'One thousand dollars is more'n I'm prepared to pay,' he said. 'I'll give you half that amount. Take it or leave it.'

'An' if I leave it?'

'I'll hand you over to Jake an' chance that he does succeed in beatin' the truth outa you.'

Ollie Prout frowned. He had assumed that Cheney would bargain and had hoped that the payment agreed would be rather more than half his initial demand. But he was no fool and quickly realized that the saloon-keeper was unlikely to budge.

'OK,' he said reluctantly. 'It's a deal.'

Leroy Cheney smiled and, rising from his seat, went across to where a large, solid-looking safe stood in the corner of the room. He twiddled with the combination lock and swung open the heavy iron door. From inside he extracted a large wad of ten-dollar dollar bills, which he proceeded to count out in piles of ten. When he had five piles on the desk before him, he returned the remainder of the notes to the safe and locked it shut. Thereupon, he resumed his seat and swept the five small separate piles into one.

Prout made to lift the $500 off the desk, but Cheney grabbed him by the wrist.

'The money's yours,' said Cheney, '*after* you tell me what you know.'

The homesteader gasped as the other held him in a vice-like grip.

'Start talkin',' growled the saloon-keeper.

'OK! OK! Jest let go of me, will you?'

Cheney glowered at Prout and shook his head.

'You want me to break your goddam wrist, then keep on prevaricatin',' he hissed.

Ollie Prout knew when he was beaten. And, so, still grimacing with pain, he began, 'Sheriff Beau Flanders told Stone he'd be prepared to move against you provided he received written complaints from some of the folk who you've been forcin' to pay tribute.' Prout smiled nervously and went on, 'I was one of those Stone approached. He gave me an affidavit to sign.'

'But you refused?'

'Nope. I signed it.'

'You did what?'

'It was to fool him into believin' I was as keen as the others to be rid of you.'

'But you figured you'd make yourself a few dollars by spillin' the beans to me, enough for you to move on an' start afresh. Is that it?'

'Yeah. That's right.'

'I see. So, who else signed?'

'I dunno, though Stone did say that he was aimin' to collect six complaints altogether.'

Scowling darkly, Leroy Cheney pushed the pile of ten-dollar bills across his desk towards the homesteader. Prout grabbed the money and thrust it into his coat pocket. Then he made as though to leave.

'Sit down!' snapped Cheney.

'But — '

'Sit down!'

Prout reluctantly did as he was bid.

'Now,' said Cheney, 'let's figure out what to do.'

'Stone's sure to be stayin' with his buddy, the Reverend,' growled Jake Inglis. 'So, how's about me an' the boys headin' on over there an' shootin' 'em up? Then we can grab hold of the affidavits an' set light to 'em.'

'What about the Reverend an' his family?' said Cheney. 'If'n there's a shoot-out, they could git caught in the crossfire.'

'That's a chance we'll have to take, Leroy.'

'No. The Reverend or any of his family gits killed an' we surely will have Beau Flanders on our necks.'

'Then, whaddya suggest?'

'Let me think.'

The saloon-keeper leant back in his chair, closed his eyes and began stroking his neat pencil-thin moustache. Meanwhile, Ollie Prout and Jake Inglis remained silently waiting.

At last Cheney opened his eyes and smiled.

'I got it, Jake,' he said. 'It's simple. What we do is take out Coyote Kate an' trade her life for them there affidavits.'

'You think Stone will buy that?'

'Sure he will. An', even if'n he ain't keen to trade, I'm sure the Reverend and that cowboy will persuade him to play along.'

'Yeah, I guess so.'

'Therefore, Jake, when you an' the

boys grab Coyote, make darned sure you take her alive. Dead, she ain't no use to us.'

'You can rely on me, Leroy.'

Ollie Prout coughed nervously.

'I reckon you ain't gonna need me any more, so I'll jest mosey along,' he mumbled.

'Oh, but we do need you!' said Cheney.

'You do?'

'Yeah. Once Jake an' the boys have captured Coyote, I propose to call on the Reverend with my ultimatum. I don't expect he'll agree straight away. So, I'll give him, Stone an' the cowboy jest twelve hours to comply. If they haven't handed over them six affidavits by then, the girl dies.' Cheney smiled thinly and added, 'Meantime, we'll need to keep her hidden somewhere outa the way. I reckon your homestead would be the ideal spot.'

Jake Inglis nodded his agreement.

'Good thinkin', Leroy,' he growled. 'If Stone an' the others come lookin' for

Coyote, they are sure to head for this here saloon. They'll never suspect she's bein' held out at Prout's homestead.'

'But I cain't be responsible for that li'l hellcat!' expostulated Prout in alarm.

'We'll tie her to a chair,' said Inglis.

'Even so, I don't think . . . '

'Come, come, Mr Prout,' said Cheney. 'There is no need to panic. We'll leave Roy Davin an' Timmy Tinker at the homestead, to keep you company an' act as her jailers. Now, I cain't say fairer than that.'

'Er . . . no, no, I s'pose not.'

''Course not.' Cheney turned to his cousin and said, 'Once I've got hold of an' destroyed the affidavits, I suggest, Jake, that you an' the boys escort Stone an' the cowboy outa town. An' make certain they take the fork in the trail that leads south.'

'Will do.'

'OK, go round up the boys an' ride out to Coyote Kate's place. You go with 'em, Mr Prout.'

'But — '

'I ain't askin'. I'm tellin' you,' said Cheney, fixing the homesteader with a basilisk stare.

'Ah, I see! OK, then, Mr Cheney, I'll . . . er . . . be goin',' stammered Ollie Prout, and he quickly followed Jake Inglis out of the saloon-keeper's office.

Behind them, Leroy Cheney stubbed out his cigar and proceeded to light a fresh one.

Jake Inglis waited until the latest hand at the blackjack table was completed. Then, with a jerk of his thumb, he indicated that Timmy Tinker, Roy Davin, Red Burton and Roscoe Jonson should vacate their seats. Sensing that something was amiss, the four shootists made no protest, but simply rose and followed their leader out of the saloon. Ollie Prout reluctantly brought up the rear.

Minutes later, they were riding out of town and cantering along the snow-covered trail in the direction of Coyote Kate Driscoll's one-time horse ranch. Inglis had briefly explained to his gang what needed to be done and had emphasized that Coyote Kate must be taken alive.

They passed Ollie Prout's homestead and then, upon reaching the bounds of the girl's ranch, Inglis raised his arm and brought them to a halt. He eyed the ranch house standing a hundred yards off, with the light spilling out from its windows.

'OK, boys,' he said, 'let's make darned sure that li'l hellcat don't give us the slip.'

'Wa'al, guess she's in the house,' stated Roy Davin. 'There ain't no light anywhere else.'

'That's right, Roy. So, what I suggest is this: we circle the house an' Red an' Roscoe cover either end. Then, once they're in place, you an' Timmy force an entry at the rear, an' me, I'll barge in through the front door. That way, we should cover every possible escape route.'

'Er . . . what about me?' enquired Ollie Prout.

'You stay put out front. Once we've got hold of Coyote, you, together with Roy an' Timmy, will escort her to your homestead, where you'll keep her prisoner until Leroy an' I git them six affidavits off Stone an' the Reverend.' Inglis glanced at each of the others in turn. 'Is that clear to all of you?' he barked.

'Sure is,' replied Roy Davin.

The rest of the gang responded in grunts and muttered affirmatives. Only Ollie Prout said nothing. He was none too happy with his role. When he had informed Leroy Cheney of Stone's plan, he had not expected to be involved in Cheney's attempt to thwart it.

'OK. Then let's get goin',' said Inglis.

They left the trail and rode through the gateway, with its ancient wooden sign proclaiming, DRISCOLL'S HORSE RANCH. Then they spread out and, upon reaching the ranch house, proceeded to surround it.

Jake Inglis waited until Red Burton and Roscoe Jonson had stationed themselves at either end of the house. Thereupon, he dismounted, drew his Colt Peacemaker and climbed up on to the stoop. He turned the door-handle and was about to push open the front door and barge in when the sudden blast of a shotgun caused him to stop in his tracks.

Roy Davin and Timmy Tinker also hesitated outside the rear door.

What had happened was simple. Coyote Kate had been about to go out and feed her grey mare when, on glancing out of the window, she had spotted the group of horsemen gathered together close beside the gateway to her property. Then, with mounting concern, she had observed them ride through the gateway and head towards the ranch house.

Quickly, she had grabbed down the shotgun from its resting-place on the rear wall of the cabin. Since that day in June, when Inglis and his gang had driven off her horses, Kate had kept the gun loaded. She rammed some extra shells into the pocket of her denims and hurried across to the nearest window, which she promptly threw open. As she did so, Red Burton appeared outside. Kate didn't hesitate. She aimed, cocked and fired the shotgun. The ten-gauge shot struck the shootist in the chest and toppled him from his horse.

As he cried out and as Jake Inglis, Roy Davin and Timmy Tinker, following their initial hesitation, charged into the ranch house, Kate threw her shotgun through the open window and then dived out after it. She retrieved the weapon, stepped over the fallen and groaning form of the wounded gunslinger and swiftly mounted his horse. Thereupon, she turned the beast's head and set off at a gallop towards her gateway and the trail beyond.

Behind her, Jake Inglis and his gang were thrown into some confusion. Finding the cabin empty, Inglis and the other two turned on their heels and dashed back outside. Roscoe Jonson, meantime, had ridden round to the opposite side of the cabin and dismounted to tend to his stricken comrade, while Ollie Prout sat motionless and dumbstruck as Kate galloped past him.

She had disappeared into the darkness before the homesteader eventually recovered his wits. Then he yelled, 'Fellers, the hellcat's made a break for it!'

'Which way did she go?' demanded a furious Jake Inglis.

'Thataway. Towards town,' replied Prout.

'Then let's git after her,' rasped Inglis.

'What about Red?' enquired Roscoe Jonson.

'You take care of him. Coyote usually rides into Horseshoe Bend on a buckboard. You can lay Red out on that an' drive him into town to see the doc,' replied Inglis, before adding brusquely, 'Meantime, the rest of you will ride with me. An' that means you, too, Prout.'

While Red Burton lay bleeding on the ground and Roscoe Jonson attempted to stanch the blood seeping from the various buckshot wounds in the shootist's chest, Jake Inglis and the rest of the gang swiftly mounted their horses and, together with a reluctant Ollie Prout, set off in pursuit of the girl.

Ahead of them, Kate galloped at full speed towards the town. In her haste to escape, she had automatically headed in that direction. Now she reflected that she might have done better had she made for the hills, for she could expect no protection from the law in the person of Marshal Bill Murray. Jack Stone and the young Texan, Pete Redford, would doubtless come to her aid, but they were probably to be found at the pastor's home, and Kate had no wish to lead Jake Inglis and his gang there. In any resultant gun-battle, Hannah or her children might easily get shot, which was something that Kate could not, would not, let happen.

Consequently, upon crossing the

town limits and entering a dark and deserted Main Street, the girl looked about her anxiously, desperately seeking another avenue of escape. Most shops, stores and houses had their shutters closed or their curtains drawn. The Horseshoe Bend Hotel and the Black Stallion saloon were two of the very few places still to have light spilling out on to the sidewalk. In an instant, Kate determined to slip down the alley between the hotel and the stage-line depot.

She attempted an abrupt turn into this alleyway, but her horse slipped and fell in the muddy quagmire that was Main Street. Kate was thrown sideways as the horse fell and she narrowly escaped being crushed by the animal. At the same time, she lost her grip of the shotgun, which flew off in the opposite direction, landing in the shadows beside the sidewalk.

Although shocked and dazed, Kate scrambled to her feet. In the darkness, she was unable to see the gun lying only a few yards away. And she had no time to search for it, for her pursuers were by now close on her tail. Her horse had fortunately suffered no serious injury and it, too, scrambled to its feet. The girl grabbed hold of the bridle and hastily swung herself back into the saddle.

But she was too late. The mishap had allowed her pursuers to catch up with her. Consequently, as she regained her seat, the foremost of them drew alongside and grabbed hold of her. He was none other than the huge, heavily bearded Roy Davin. This giant of a man had little trouble in lifting the girl bodily from her horse and clasping her in his bear-like embrace. Her struggles were hopeless. She was held fast.

Jake Inglis, Timmy Tinker and Ollie Prout rode up as the girl began to scream for help. Her screams were short-lived, for Jake Inglis leant across and rammed the muzzle of his Colt Peacemaker hard into Kate's ribs.

'Shuddup or I'll shoot you dead!' he snarled.

Kate's screams died away.

'Wh . . . what d'you want with me?' she demanded in a low voice.

'We're lookin' for a hostage,' explained Inglis.

'A hostage! But why?'

'We're aimin' to exchange you for a bunch of affidavits your pals are intendin' to show to Sheriff Flanders over in Elk City.'

'How'd you know 'bout that?' Kate glared at the gunslinger, then suddenly glimpsed Ollie Prout mounted directly behind him. She peered hard at the homesteader through the darkness until she was sure that he was indeed her neighbour. 'You!' she cried. 'You betrayed us, you goddam snake in the grass!'

'I told you to shuddup,' hissed Jake Inglis.

'Yeah. If'n she don't button her lips, knock her teeth out,' said Prout.

Jake Inglis turned in the saddle and

coldly eyed the homesteader.

'You can shuddup, too,' he sneered contemptuously. 'Coyote's right. You are a goddam snake in the grass.'

'I served you well. If I hadn't spilled the beans to Mr Cheney, you'd be in big trouble,' protested Prout.

'Mebbe so. Anyways, Roy, you an' Timmy take the girl out to Prout's place an' keep her locked up there. Prout, you ride with 'em.'

Prout made no response, but turned his horse's head, ready to return in the direction from which they had come. At the same time, Timmy Tinker grasped hold of the bridle of Kate's horse and brought it across to stand between his pinto and Roy Davin's gelding.

'I'm gonna put you back on your hoss,' Davin rasped into the girl's ear. 'An' then we're gonna ride nice'n steady out to Prout's homestead. You try shoutin', or anythin' else, an' I'll start breakin' bones. You got that, Coyote?'

'Got it,' muttered Kate through clenched teeth.

'Good!'

The giant gunslinger heaved the girl back into the saddle and, with Ollie Prout leading and himself and Timmy Tinker riding on either side of their prisoner, they set off back along Main Street in the direction of the homestead.

'See you later, boys,' said Jake Inglis.

He watched them go and then, as they vanished into the darkness, he wheeled round and headed for Doc Shaw's surgery. He dismounted, climbed up on to the sidewalk and knocked upon the doctor's door.

'This is kinda late to be callin',' said Doc Shaw grumpily, when eventually he opened the door. 'Cain't it wait till mornin'?'

'No, it cain't,' Inglis informed him. 'Red Burton's got hisself shot full of buckshot an' needs tendin' to.'

Doc Shaw did his best to contain his glee at hearing this piece of news, but was unable to erase his smile completely.

'How come such a peaceable feller got himself shot?' he enquired ironically.

'That ain't none of your darned business,' retorted Inglis. 'Jest you be ready to treat him. He'll be along here directly.'

'It'll be a pleasure to pull the buckshot outa him,' said the doctor.

'Right, I'll mosey along then,' said Inglis, discomfited by Doc Shaw's evident delight at the shooting of his comrade.

He turned and, watched by a cheerfully smiling Doc Shaw, unhitched his horse and led it across the street to the Black Stallion, where he again hitched it, this time to the rail outside that saloon.

The bar-room remained much as it had been when Jake Inglis and his gang had left earlier. Inglis felt badly in need of a drink, but decided to postpone pushing his way through the mêlée of drinkers round the bar until after he had reported to his cousin. He found Leroy Cheney still seated behind the desk in his office, smoking a fresh cigar and with a bottle of his best Tennessee whiskey in front of him. There were two glasses, one half-full and the other empty. The saloon-keeper pushed the empty glass across the table towards Jake Inglis.

'Help yourself, Jake,' said Cheney.

'Thanks, Leroy.'

The big gunslinger poured himself a generous measure, then seated himself opposite his cousin and lifted the glass to his lips. The amber liquid slid down his throat and, as he felt the warmth spread up from his stomach, he sighed contentedly.

'Good stuff, eh?' said Cheney.

'Sure is. The best,' affirmed Inglis.

'So, how'd it go, Jake?' asked the saloon-keeper.

'It could've gone better,' confessed Inglis. 'Red got hisself shot up.'

'An' Coyote Kate?'

'We got her. In the end.' Inglis took another gulp of whiskey and proceeded to relate what had happened. He finished by saying, 'Roy an' Timmy will make darned sure Coyote don't escape from Ollie Prout's place.'

Leroy Cheney nodded.

'You did well,' he informed his cousin. Red Burton's mishap was unfortunate, yet it did not unduly concern him. Indeed, Cheney's only concern had been that Coyote Kate might elude them. 'With that li'l hellcat under lock an' key, I reckon we're holdin' all the aces,' he concluded.

'Yup.'

'So, Jake, once we've knocked back these here whiskeys, I suggest we pay the Reverend Dunwoody a visit.'

Both men grinned and raised their glasses.

# 8

Supper had finished in the pastor's house and Hannah was upstairs saying goodnight to her two children when there came a knocking on the front door. The Reverend Daniel Dunwoody excused himself and, leaving Jack Stone and Pete Redford seated in his comfortable parlour, went to answer the door. Upon opening it, he found himself confronted by the elegant, immaculately clad figure of Leroy Cheney and his rough, tough cousin, the formidable Jake Inglis.

' 'Evenin', Reverend,' Cheney greeted the pastor.

'Good evening, Mr Cheney, Mr Inglis,' Dunwoody replied politely. 'To what do I owe the pleasure of this call?'

'We got somethin' to put to you, Reverend. Ain't that so, Jake?' said Cheney.

'Yup, we sure have,' agreed Inglis.

'Then you'd best come in,' said Dunwoody.

The smug look on Cheney's face and the ugly leer on that of his cousin worried the pastor. Earlier, Dunwoody had entertained high hopes that Leroy Cheney's reign of terror might soon be ended. Now, he feared that his optimism could have been misplaced. He sensed that the saloon-keeper was about to spring a nasty surprise.

Cheney and Inglis followed the pastor through into the parlour, where they found Stone and Redford. Cheney regarded the Kentuckian and the young Texan with a contemptuous eye and murmured silkily, 'Wa'al, wa'al, ain't this nice'n cosy?'

'You wantin' somethin'?' rasped Stone.

'Mr Cheney says he has something he wishes to put to me,' said Dunwoody.

'To put to all of you,' said Cheney.

'Oh, yeah?' growled Stone.

'Yes. A proposition.'

'Go on,' said Dunwoody, his feeling of alarm increasing as he studied the triumphant expression on the other's countenance.

'It's like this, Reverend, a li'l bird told me that your friends have been kinda busy collectin' complaints against me. Seems you have six signed affidavits, which you intend handin' in to Sheriff Beau Flanders over in Elk City. But this don't worry me in the least.'

'It doesn't?'

'No, Reverend, it don't. Y'see, the sheriff ain't gonna git them affidavits, 'cause you're gonna hand them over to me.'

'And why should I do that?'

''Cause if'n you don't, your li'l friend, Coyote Kate, is gonna die.'

'You've got Kate?'

'I certainly have.'

The colour drained from Dunwoody's face and he turned anxiously to the Kentuckian.

'What on earth do we do, Jack?' he sighed.

'There ain't no easy answer to that,' growled Stone.

'We cain't let Kate die!' exclaimed Redford.

'But, if we hand over the affidavits, the complainants . . . ' began Stone.

'I give you my word that all that'll happen to 'em is that I'll increase the amount of tribute they pay,' said Cheney. 'Hell, that's only fair!'

'You won't hurt them?' enquired Dunwoody.

'No, Reverend, I won't hurt them.'

'We need time to think this over,' declared Stone.

Cheney smiled coldly, removed the fob-watch from his vest-pocket and studied it.

'It's exactly nine-fifteen,' he said. 'I'll be generous an' give you twelve hours.' He pointed at Stone and Redford and continued, 'I want you two to report tomorrow mornin' at the Black Stallion with them six affidavits. An' you be there sharp at a quarter past nine.'

'If'n we do, you'll release Kate?' said Redford.

'Yup. An' you'll both leave town. Only, this time, you won't be comin' back. OK?'

'OK,' said Stone.

'In that case, I'll bid you good evenin', but I'll expect to see you on Christmas Eve mornin',' stated the saloon-keeper.

So saying, Cheney turned on his heel and, followed by his cousin, marched out of the house. The front door had scarcely closed behind them when Hannah came downstairs and rejoined the others.

'What did those two want?' she demanded, for she had observed the two men arrive from one of the upstairs bedroom windows.

Daniel Dunwoody explained briefly the purpose of their call and concluded, 'I do not see how we can abandon Kate to her fate, yet, should we hand Cheney those affidavits, we would be betraying the six brave people who signed them.'

'The five brave people,' Stone corrected him.

'I beg your pardon, but there were six.'

'One of whom has betrayed us.'

'You don't know that, Jack.'

'It's gotta be. Who else knew 'bout the affidavits? Only Sam Flanagan, an' I cain't believe he'd betray us.'

'That's right. It has to be one of 'em,' said Redford.

'But which one?' asked Hannah.

'There's the rub. How do we find out?' muttered the pastor.

'Cheney knew that there are six affidavits,' said Stone. 'So, Pete, did you mention how many we were collectin' to Mr Black, or Mr Brady, or Mr Newton?'

'Nope,' said Redford. 'I know I mentioned that there were other complainants, yet I'm darned sure I didn't tell none of 'em that they numbered six.'

'I did mention that fact,' said Stone, 'but only to one of my three. I remember distinctly. Ollie Prout asked point blank how many signatures I was collectin'. I told him six, includin' his own.'

'Ollie Prout!' exclaimed Dunwoody.

'I never did take to the man,' said Hannah. 'A surly, mean-spirited feller.'

'Yes, that's true,' said Dunwoody. 'Even so, why would he betray us? Surely it was in his interests to be rid of Leroy Cheney? He was paying tribute the same as the others.'

'So, what did he hope to gain from tellin' Cheney?' growled Stone.

'Enough to quit Horseshoe Bend an' set hisself up some place else,' suggested Redford.

'Certainly, he could only be scraping a living on that homestead of his,' remarked Hannah.

'So, what *do* we do?' demanded Dunwoody.

'Wa'al, we sure as hell don't betray the other signatories,' said Stone. 'Nope, what we do is rescue Coyote Kate.'

'But how? We don't know where she's being held.'

'We can guess, Daniel.'

'I s'pose the most likely place is the Black Stallion,' commented Redford.

'You can't hope to spring her from there,' said Dunwoody. 'You're good with a gun, Jack, heaven knows. But even you can't expect to out-shoot Cheney and the rest of them.'

'That's right. Apart from Leroy Cheney, the other five are all professional gunslingers,' said Hannah.

'I'll go with Jack,' volunteered Redford. 'I can shoot a gun.'

The pastor considered the young Texan with a kindly eye. He smiled wryly and remarked, 'Hannah and I could probably shoot a gun. All you've got to do is pull the trigger. However, I doubt if we'd hit what we were aiming at.'

'Are you sayin' . . . ?'

'You are a cowboy, Pete. Not a shootist.'

'That don't mean I cain't shoot straight.'

'Do you honestly believe you could out-draw any one of the Inglis gang?'

'I dunno.'

'Wa'al, I do,' said Stone. 'Daniel's right We wouldn't stand a chance goin' agin' the six of' em.'

'Perhaps you won't have to,' said Hannah.

'Whaddya mean?'

'I mean, Jack, that I don't think Cheney is holding Kate at the Black Stallion.'

Stone eyed his friend's wife with some interest. He was beginning to realize that Hannah was not merely a pretty face.

'Why wouldn't he hold her there?' he growled.

'Leroy Cheney won't want a gunfight in his saloon. Why would he?'

'Wa'al, I can see why he wouldn't,' Stone conceded.

'You go barging in there and he will, in all probability, stand back and let you search the place from top to bottom. Then, when you fail to find Kate, he'll simply laugh in your face and repeat the ultimatum he gave you earlier.'

'OK. S'pose you're right, where *do* you reckon he's holdin' Kate?'

'At Ollie Prout's homestead.'

The Kentuckian whistled. That possibility had not occurred to him.

'Certainly, Cheney ain't likely to suspect that we know it was Prout who betrayed us.' he said.

'An' Prout's place is ideal, bein' outa the way like it is,' said Redford. 'So, let's git out there.'

'You'll need to be careful,' said Hannah, 'for I don't expect that Cheney has left Ollie Prout to look after Kate on his own. He's sure to have dispatched one or two of his gang to keep Prout company.'

'I think we can handle a coupla them no-good critters, cain't we, Pete?' drawled the Kentuckian.

'Sure thing, Jack. After all, we're gonna have the element of surprise on our side,' said Redford eagerly.

'I feel you should also have the law

on your side,' interjected Dunwoody.

'How d'you mean?' enquired Stone.

'You should enlist the marshal to go with you.'

'Are you kiddin'? He's in Leroy Cheney's pocket.'

'Bill Murray is a good man, Jack. I told you that already. Perhaps this is the chance he's been waiting for, actually to stand up to Cheney and his gang?' suggested Dunwoody.

'Could be, I s'pose,' muttered the Kentuckian.

'Well, are you going to try to enlist his help?' asked Hannah.

Stone pondered this question for some moments.

'I guess so,' he said eventually.

The two men left the house, saddled their horses and led them out of the pastor's stables. They crossed the street and made their way behind the church. To avoid any chance of being spotted by the enemy, they intended approaching the law office from the rear. They mounted their horses and proceeded on a parallel course to Main Street until they reached the back of the law office. The cells were at the rear and, beneath the stars, the sight of the barred windows told them that they had reached their goal.

There was a side-door, which, much to their surprise, Stone and Redford found unlocked. Stone flung it open and they stepped inside to find themselves standing in a narrow corridor along which were the law office's three cells. None of these cells was occupied.

They passed along the corridor towards the connecting door between it and the front office. This, too, Stone flung open. Marshal Bill Murray was alone in the office. He was seated behind his desk and looked up in surprise at their unexpected entry.

''Evenin', Marshal,' said Stone quietly. 'Kinda careless of you to leave your side-door open, wasn't it?'

'My deppity Joe slipped out to grab hisself some supper. Guess he didn't bother to lock it, seein' as we ain't holdin' no prisoners at present,' replied the marshal. 'Anyways, what can I do for you two gents?'

'You can help us release Coyote Kate.'

'Whaddya mean? Who's holdin' her?'

'Some of Jake Inglis's gang, we reckon.'

'Where?'

'Out at Ollie Prout's place.'

'An' why would they do that?'

Slowly, yet succinctly, Stone explained to the marshal about the six affidavits and how Kate was being held hostage until they were handed over to Leroy Cheney. He concluded by saying, 'Me an' Pete want you along as the supposed upholder of the law round here.'

'You crazy? We go up agin' the Inglis gang, we'll git ourselves killed for sure.'

'We ain't goin' up agin' the entire Inglis gang. I figure there'll be one, or mebbe two at most, out there keepin' an eye on Kate. The Reverend says you were a good lawman once. Wa'al, I'm givin' you the chance to prove it.'

'You owe it to yourself, to your family, 'deed to everybody, to take this chance,' interjected Redford.

'That's right,' said Stone. 'It's time to stand up an' be counted, Marshal.'

Bill Murray reflected on this. He had been a good town marshal up until the arrival of Cheney and his associates back in the spring. And he was a proud man. It had hurt him to submit to the saloon-keeper's demands and let Jake Inglis and his gang ride roughshod over the citizens of Horseshoe Bend. But he had felt powerless to oppose them. He could have taken his wife and family with him and quit town. That, though, would have been the coward's way out. Consequently, he had stayed and done his best to curb Cheney to some extent, and to maintain at least a modicum of law and order.

'You've got quite a reputation, Mr Stone,' he said. 'So, I reckon I'd be a darned fool not to step up alongside you an' your pardner.'

166

'Good man!' said Stone. 'But, before we set out, you'd best swear in Pete an' me as deppities, for we wanta keep this nice an' legal.'

Bill Murray smiled wearily.

'I can do that, but I ain't got no spare badges,' he replied.

'I don't figure we need badges, do we, Pete?' growled Stone.

'No, Jack, I guess not,' said the young Texan.

And so Marshal Bill Murray swore them in as deputies and then wrote a note for his deputy, Joe Dunn, which he left on his desk. It read as follows:

*Some important business has just come up. I'll explain when I return. Meantime, you are in charge of the office.*
                                              *Bill*

'That should do,' he said. 'Now I'll fetch my horse.'

'Fine. Meet us out back,' said Stone.

The ride out to Ollie Prout's homestead was made in silence and they encountered nobody on the trail between the town and their destination. Upon arrival, the three men dismounted and hitched their horses to Prout's boundary fence. Then they stepped on to his property and cautiously approached the house. The snow muffled the sound of their footsteps and they reached the stoop without discovery. There they halted and crouched down in its shadow.

'I'll go see what's what 'fore we make any move,' whispered Stone.

'OK,' replied the marshal, while Pete Redford merely nodded.

Stone slowly, stealthily, mounted the steps on to the stoop. Although a big man, he moved with the grace of a mountain lion. His years as an Army scout had taught him how to glide across the ground almost as silently as an Apache or Kiowa brave. And nobody, but nobody, matched them for their ability to advance upon their enemy both unseen and unheard.

The Kentuckian crossed the stoop

and bent down low beside the nearest window. He raised his head a few inches and peered in. He took in the whole scene in one swift glance and then promptly dropped down beneath the level of the window-sill.

Coyote Kate Driscoll was seated on a straight-backed kitchen chair, bound hand and foot, yet not gagged. She sat to one side of the fireplace, in which a meagre fire burned. On the opposite side sat Roy Davin, drinking coffee and talking to Timmy Tinker, who was seated at the kitchen table and smoking a cheroot. Ollie Prout, meantime, also sat at the kitchen table, where he was reading the latest edition of Fred Newton's Horseshoe Bend *Chronicle*.

Stone crept round to the rear of the house and found another door. He tried turning the handle and eased the door open a fraction of an inch. Then he quietly closed it. He knew now what they must do.

Upon rejoining the others, Stone addressed them in a whisper.

'There are three of 'em in there with Kate: Ollie Prout an' two of Jake Inglis's gang,' he said. 'An' we gotta git them 'fore they can grab Kate an' use her as a shield or a hostage.'

'An' jest how do we manage that?' asked the marshal.

'There's an unlocked door at the back,' said Stone. 'You give me a coupla minutes to reach that there door an' then you barge in through the front one. You'll find Ollie Prout an' one of the shootists sittin' at the kitchen table directly in front of you. Beyond the table is the fireplace, with Kate seated on the left an' the other shootist on the right of it. I'll enter from the rear an' take care of the shootist nearest the fireplace. Marshal, you take care of the shootist at the table, an' Pete, you take care of Prout. Got it?'

'Got it,' said Redford and Murray in unison.

Stone clapped each man on the shoulder and then silently made his way once again round the side of the house to the rear.

This time Stone didn't hesitate, but threw open the back door and leapt inside. He found himself standing in a short passage, with what he assumed were bedchambers on either side. Ahead of him stood another door. He reached this in a couple of bounds, hurled it open and stormed into the main room of the house. As he did so, Marshal Bill Murray burst in through the front door, closely followed by Pete Redford.

'What the hell!' exclaimed Roy Davin.

He quickly transferred the mug of coffee from his right to his left hand, and then attempted to draw the Colt Peacemaker from its holster. But he was too late. Jack Stone's Frontier Model Colt was already in the big Kentuckian's hand and blazing fire. One, two, three, the bullets slammed into Davin. The first hit him in the chest, smashing through his ribs and ripping into his black heart, the second struck him in the throat and the third entered the centre of his forehead and exploded inside his skull. The giant gunslinger was hurled backwards with such force that, when he hit the floor, the windows rattled and the whole building seemed to shake.

Meantime, Timmy Tinker and Ollie Prout had leapt up from where they sat at the kitchen table.

Tinker, like Davin, made to draw his revolver. The Remington quickly cleared leather and was raised and pointing at the marshal when Murray fired. The slug struck Tinker in the shoulder and spun him round He screamed and dropped his gun. It skeetered across the floor in the direction of the Kentuckian. Tinker dived after the gun and, stretching out his left hand, tried to grab hold of it. The shootist's fingers closed round the butt in the same instant that Jack Stone stamped his foot down on top of them. Tinker screamed a second time and promptly released his grip on the gun, which Stone kicked aside.

Stone turned to Pete Redford.

'You got Prout covered, I see,' he remarked.

'Yeah. The yeller bastard didn't offer no resistance at all,' said the young Texan.

This was true. Ollie Prout did not carry a weapon, nor did he make any attempt to grab one, although there were both a shotgun and a rifle hanging on his wall. Instead, before Redford could even bring his Colt Peacemaker to bear on him, the homesteader leapt to his feet and thrust his hands up into the air.

'I . . . I didn't want no part in this!' he cried. 'They made me go along with them.'

'You liar! You betrayed us to Cheney,' said Stone.

'No. Really. I dunno what you're talkin' about. I — '

'When you fellers've quite finished gabbin',' Coyote Kate interrupted him,

'I'd sure be obliged if'n you would cut me free.'

Pete Redford grinned and stepped across to where the girl sat, bound hand and foot on a kitchen chair, to one side of the fireplace. He pulled a knife from its sheath at his waist and proceeded to slice through both sets of bonds.

'There,' he said. 'How's that?'

Kate smiled gratefully at him and began to rub life back into her wrists and arms.

'Better. Much better,' she gasped.

While Kate progressed from her wrists and arms to her ankles and legs, Jack Stone dragged Timmy Tinker to his feet. He was none too gentle and the shootist cried out in anguish as the Kentuckian grasped him by the arm and twisted it up behind his wounded shoulder. Then Stone twisted Tinker's other arm up beside the first.

'You got any handcuffs with you, Marshal?' he enquired.

Bill Murray shook his head.

'Wa'al, it don't matter. We can use

that rope the sonsofbitches used to bind Kate,' said Stone.

Murray picked up a length of rope from the floor and bound the gunslinger's wrists together. He was no gentler than Stone had been and Tinker suffered considerable pain during the course of this. He did not suffer in silence, however. When he was eventually securely bound, Stone turned to the homesteader.

'Now it's your turn,' he rasped.

'I'm tellin' you I'm innocent!' protested Ollie Prout.

'He's lyin',' said Kate.

'Yeah. We know he is,' said Pete Redford. 'He told Cheney 'bout the affidavits an', as a result, Cheney decided to take you hostage, to be exchanged for 'em.'

'No, I didn't! I swear I didn't!' cried Prout.

'There are six signatories,' said Stone. 'Cheney knew that. Of the six, only you were given that information.'

'Oh!'

The colour drained from Ollie Prout's face and he fell silent.

'OK, let's git these two back to the law office an' stick 'em in the cells,' said Stone. Then he glanced at the bloodied corpse of Roy Davin and added, 'We can ask Ben Brady to pick up the body later.'

The two prisoners had to be helped on to their horses. Mounting, with their hands tied behind their backs, would have been impossible unaided. They made no attempt to ride off while Stone and the others climbed into the saddle. Timmy Tinker was too badly wounded and Ollie Prout was too scared to try any such thing.

The ride back into town was made without incident. The horses were hitched to the rail outside the law office and then the prisoners were marched inside, where they were greeted by Bill Murray's deputy, Joe Dunn.

The deputy was a small, heavily bewhiskered gnome of a man in his mid-forties, honest and dependable, but no leader of men. He had also been deputy to Bill Murray's predecessor.

'What in tarnation is goin' on, Marshal?' he exclaimed.

'We are somewhat belatedly takin' action agin' Leroy Cheney an' his associates,' stated Murray. 'So, lock these two no-account critters in the cells, will you, Joe?'

'OK, Marshal. It'll be my pleasure,' said Dunn gleefully.

The others waited until the deputy had locked the two miscreants in one of the cells and returned. Thereupon, Marshal Bill Murray addressed all of them.

'Since Cheney's arrival in town last spring, law an' order has pretty well ceased to exist here in Horseshoe Bend,' he said. 'This ain't somethin' I'm partickerly proud of.'

'Nor me,' added Joe Dunn.

'Me an' Joe, we've done what we could to preserve the peace,' said the marshal. 'But there was no way we could take on Cheney an' the Inglis gang an' hope to win. Now I b'lieve we can.'

''Course we can,' declared Kate eagerly. 'The Rogers brothers are dead, as is Roy Davin. Timmy Tinker is behind bars an' Red Burton ain't exactly fightin' fit, not after me pepperin' him with buckshot. Guess he'll be lyin' down nursin' his wounds some place.'

'Which leaves only three of 'em to tackle,' said Stone.

'An' Leroy Cheney ain't no hot shot with a gun,' Dunn remarked, with a grin.

'You figure you can take Jake Inglis, Mr Stone?' enquired the marshal.

'I do.'

'Good! Then I aim to take on Roscoe Jonson.'

'An' I'll go up agin' Cheney,' averred Kate.

'You gonna pepper him with buck-shot, too?' laughed Stone.

'Nope. Gimme a revolver an' I'll plug him. You jest watch me.'

'I don't think so,' said Pete Redford. 'I'll take Cheney.'

'But — '

'Kate, you're the one person in Horseshoe Bend who's stood up to Cheney an' his gang. You don't need to prove nuthin',' said Murray. 'So, leave it to me an' the others, will you?'

'What about me?' said Joe Dunn.

'Somebody's gotta mind the law office, partickerly now we've got them two prisoners back there in the cells,' replied Murray.

'I s'pose.'

'Then that's settled. Let's git goin',' said the marshal.

'I'm comin' with you,' remarked Kate.

'Hell, no!' said Stone.

'I won't git in your way, I promise. I jest wanta be there,' declared Kate.

Bill Murray sighed.

'OK. You can come,' he said. 'But you gotta stay outside the saloon till the shootin's over.'

'Fine. I'll watch events from over the

top of the batwing doors,' promised the girl meekly.

Jack Stone regarded the girl with a quizzical eye. Meek acquiescence was not something he had expected from her. He shrugged his brawny shoulders and grinned.

'Let's go,' he said.

The Kentuckian marched out of the law office and turned and headed along the sidewalk in the direction of the Black Stallion saloon. Behind him Marshal Bill Murray and Pete Redford walked side by side, while a determined-looking Coyote Kate Driscoll brought up the rear.

# 9

It being mid-week and late, the crowd in the bar-room of the Black Stallion had thinned somewhat. However, there remained a fair number of gamblers round the roulette table and, although the two games of blackjack had ended, the poker game continued. Jake Inglis and Roscoe Jonson stood at the bar drinking whiskey and smoking cheroots in company with a few late-night drinkers still scattered along its length.

As for the saloon's sporting women, three were upstairs with customers, while the fourth, who was also upstairs, was busy entertaining her employer, Leroy Cheney. In a fifth bedchamber, Red Burton, his face chalk-white and his eyes filled with pain, stretched out on a lumpy, narrow cot designed for the purpose of quick fornication rather than for a good night's sleep. Doc Shaw had removed the buckshot, with which Coyote Kate had peppered him, and had bandaged his many wounds, yet these wounds hurt every time he moved.

A three-parts empty bottle of rye whiskey stood on a low table beside the bed. A tumbler containing a generous measure of the amber liquid was clutched in Burton's right hand. It was this whiskey which was helping to dull the pain a little. But not enough, Burton contemplated, to allow him to fall asleep.

The carrot haired gunslinger was moodily musing on his situation when the door of the small bedchamber opened and the immaculately clad figure of Leroy Cheney stepped into the room.

Cheney was in a good humour. He had every confidence that the Reverend Daniel Dunwoody would hand over the six affidavits in the morning, and that the town of Horseshoe Bend would finally be rid of Jack Stone and his young Texan friend. Also, he had just experienced a most enjoyable coupling with Dolly Latimer, a voluptuous blonde who was the prettiest and sauciest of the saloon's sporting women.

'How's it goin', Red?' he enquired of his henchman.

'Not so good,' replied Burton morosely.

'No, I guess not.' Cheney threw the other a sympathetic smile. 'You're still in some considerable pain, I s'pose?'

'I sure am.'

'Cain't the doc give you somethin' to ease it?'

'He prescribed morphine, but the dose he gave me seems to have worn off. Anyways, this'll suffice till mornin',' said Red Burton, raising the tumbler and swallowing a large draught of the whiskey.

Leroy Cheney grinned.

'If'n you say so.'

' 'Sides, while I ain't sleepin', I'm thinkin' of what I'm gonna do to Coyote when I'm up an' about again,' said Burton, with an evil gleam in his eye. 'I s'pose you caught her?' he asked.

Again Leroy Cheney grinned.

'We sure did, Red,' he said. 'We're holdin' her out at Ollie Prout's place. Didn't you pass Roy an' Timmy an' the girl on their way out there as you an' Roscoe returned to town?'

Red Burton shook his head.

'Nope. I must've passed out. 'Deed, I don't recall much of anythin' till I woke up in the doc's surgery. Then I was transferred across to this here room, with Dolly keepin' watch over me. She fetched me the whiskey an' left.'

'Yeah. Wa'al, we got Coyote an' we're aimin' to exchange her for them affidavits the Reverend's holdin'.'

'Good! An' when — '

But Red Burton never completed his sentence, for, at that moment, the first of several shots rang out in the bar-room below.

★   ★   ★

While the saloon-keeper and the wounded gunslinger were talking upstairs, Jack

Stone and the others had arrived on the stoop outside the saloon. They paused before the batwing doors.

'OK,' said Stone. 'Let's see what's goin' on.'

He peered over the top of the batwing doors and slowly surveyed the scene inside the bar-room. He observed Jake Inglis and Roscoe Jonson standing at the bar-counter and noted that Leroy Cheney and Red Burton were nowhere to be seen. While the Kentuckian had not expected to see Burton, he was a little put out to find Cheney missing.

Standing beside him and also surveying the scene, Marshal Bill Murray remarked angrily, 'Goddammit, there ain't no sign of that sonofabitch, Cheney!'

'Nope.'

'Mebbe he's in his office?' suggested Pete Redford.

'Hmm, that's a possibility,' said Stone, brightening. 'You can go look for him there.'

'An' jest where is his office?' asked the Texan.

'It's to the right of the bar, 'tween it an' the stage,' said Murray.

'OK. Let's step inside an' do what we gotta do,' growled Stone. Then he turned to Kate and said, 'You remain here till the shootin' is over, like the marshal told you.'

'I will,' said Kate.

The girl's uncharacteristic meekness continued to trouble Stone, but he had more important matters to worry him. Consequently, he pushed open the batwing doors and strode briskly into the bar-room, dismissing the girl from his thoughts.

Bill Murray and Pete Redford promptly followed the Kentuckian through the doors. Murray caught up with him and the two men marched purposefully, shoulder to shoulder, towards the bar. Redford, meantime, branched off and headed for the saloon-keeper's office.

At the bar, Jake Inglis and Roscoe Jonson placed their whiskeys down on the copper-topped counter and turned to face the approaching lawmen. As they did so, their fellow-drinkers hastily shuffled away from the bar, sensing what was to come and none of them wishing to become victim of a stray bullet.

The two shootists observed the determined look in both Stone's and Murray's eyes. Jake Inglis had a sudden feeling of foreboding, but shrugged it off. After all, didn't he and his cousin hold the trump card, namely Coyote Kate?

He smiled arrogantly and said, ''Evenin', Marshal, to what do we owe this visit?'

'I'm here to arrest the pair of you,' said Murray.

'On what charge, Marshal?'

'On what charges, you should've said.' Murray smiled grimly and went on, 'How's about kidnappin' an' extortion for starters?'

Jake Inglis laughed harshly.

'I dunno what you're talkin' about,' he said.

'I think you do.'

Inglis scowled and, lowering his

voice, hissed venomously, 'Whose side are you on, Murray?'

'I'm on the side of law an' order,' retorted the marshal.

'That so? Wa'al, if'n you wanta see Coyote alive an' well, you an' your buddy will back off right now. You try to arrest me an' Roscoe an' she's dead.'

'No, she ain't.'

'Y'see,' interjected Stone, 'your boys ain't holdin' her no more.'

'Whaddya mean?'

'He means, Jake, that Roy Davin's dead an' Timmy Tinker's in jail,' explained Murray.

'Holy cow!'

Jake Inglis glanced at his fellow-shootist. Roscoe Jonson bore a grim visage. Both men realized that the game was up. They had either to stand and fight, or surrender and, in due time, face trial. And neither of them wanted to hang.

The pair reached for their guns simultaneously.

Inglis, his eyes cold as ice, faced the Kentuckian. His right hand closed round the handle of his Colt Peacemaker. As he drew the gun from its holster, he aimed, cocked and fired in one smooth, lightning-quick movement. But he was an instant too late. Stone had beaten him to the draw, and Inglis was already toppling backwards when he squeezed the trigger, thus sending his shot some inches above Stone's head.

Stone had made no mistake. His aim was true. The Frontier Model Colt spat fire, and the .45 calibre slug ploughed through the centre of Inglis's brow and blasted his brains out through the back of his skull. He hit the floor with a tremendous thud and lay there, quite still.

Roscoe Jonson was by no means the quickest shootist in Jake Inglis's gang. Therefore, before he could pull his Remington clear of its holster, Marshal Bill Murray had already drawn and fired his Colt Peacemaker. The Colt blazed and Jonson stood open-mouthed as no fewer than four bullets smashed into his chest in swift succession. He was knocked backwards a good five yards, the slugs ripping through his body and exiting out of his back in a stream of blood and splintered bone. By the time he hit the floorboards his shirt was stained crimson and he was already dead.

The smell of cordite permeated the air around the bar. The roulette-wheel had ceased to rotate and the poker-players had temporarily suspended their game. A silence had fallen across the length and breadth of the bar-room.

It was broken by Pete Redford, as he emerged from Leroy Cheney's office.

'The sonofabitch ain't in there,' he announced, indicating the office with a jerk of his thumb.

'Then, where in tarnation is he?' demanded Stone.

'Mebbe he's upstairs?' suggested Murray.

As he spoke, Red Burton lurched out on to the balcony overlooking the bar-room. He was clutching his Remington revolver.

The sound of the shooting had abruptly halted his conversation with Leroy Cheney. He had clambered painfully off the narrow cot and staggered to his feet. Then he had grabbed the gun from his holster, which was hanging suspended from a bedpost.

He and Leroy Cheney had exchanged a few brief words.

'What the blue blazes is goin' on down there?'

'I dunno. Guess we'd best find out.'

'Yeah. Let's go see.'

They had left the room and headed along the corridor towards the balcony. And Cheney, crafty as ever, had taken good care that his wounded henchman should assume the lead.

Thus it was that Red Burton stumbled on to the balcony, where he grasped the rail for support and hurriedly scanned the scene below. He observed, with mounting consternation, the motionless bodies of Jake Inglis and Roscoe Jonson stretched out on the bar-room floor.

As he did so, Pete Redford glanced upward and spotted him. The Texan had drawn his revolver prior to entering Cheney's office. He quickly raised it and fired at the carrot-headed gunslinger. The shot struck the balcony rail and sent a splinter of wood whistling past Red Burton's left ear.

The shootist immediately responded with a volley of shots aimed at different targets.

The first whipped the hat off one of the poker-players' heads and buried itself in the table behind which Redford had dived for cover. Redford's reaction was closely followed by that of the poker-players, who variously dived, slipped or fell from their chairs, overturning the poker-table in the process, as they sought to scramble out of Burton's line of fire.

Red Burton's second and third shots were aimed at the marshal and the Kentuckian, who had both dropped into a crouch. Neither found its mark, one ploughing harmlessly into the bar-counter and the other into the floorboards some three feet beyond where the Kentuckian was crouching.

The next shot came from the doorway of the saloon. The petite form of Coyote Kate stood there, with a rifle raised, the stock held tight against her shoulder. She took careful aim and squeezed the trigger.

Red Burton cried out, dropped the Remington and fell backwards on to the balcony floor.

Pete Redford, who was nearest the foot of the stairway leading to the upper floor, was the first to reach the balcony. He cautiously approached the supine gunslinger, but he need not have worried. Coyote Kate's shot had struck Burton in the heart, killing him instantly.

The Texan straightened up and raised his arm.

'He's dead,' he announced.

Downstairs, the poker-players clambered slowly to their feet, as did the bartenders and everyone else. Marshal

Bill Murray mounted the stairs and began to make his way up to join Redford, while Jack Stone headed for the doorway, where Kate stood, rifle in hand.

'That was some neat shootin',' commented the Kentuckian.

'Yeah.'

'I thought you only had a shotgun,' said Stone.

'That's right,' agreed Kate.

'Then where did you git hold of that there Winchester?' enquired Stone curiously.

'When you an' the others stepped through them batwing doors, I nipped back to the law office an' grabbed the rifle outa your saddle boot,' confessed the girl, with a saucy grin.

Stone shook his head, yet smiled nonetheless.

'A smart move, as it turned out,' he commented.

'Yeah. I guess I should've finished him off back at my ranch,' she said. 'Anyways, you an' the marshal surely finished off Jake Inglis an' Roscoe Jonson. I saw that clear enough. But I didn't see no sign of that stinkin' rat, Leroy Cheney,' remarked Kate.

'No.'

'Hadn't we better go look for him?'

'Yup, we sure had.' Stone stretched out his hand and took the Winchester from the girl. 'I don't think you're gonna be needin' that no more,' he said.

'No, reckon not,' she said, handing him the rifle.

They hurried across the bar-room floor and headed upstairs. By the time they reached the balcony, both Redford and the marshal had disappeared They stepped over the corpse of Red Burton and entered the corridor beyond.

Pete Redford was taking one side of the corridor and Bill Murray the other. They were searching each bedchamber in turn. Stone and the girl waited until they had completed this task.

'Wa'al?' said the Kentuckian.

Both men shook their heads.

'He ain't up here,' said Redford. 'All the rooms are empty.'

'No, but he could easily have climbed out of a window an' dropped to the ground below,' remarked the marshal.

'What are you sayin', Marshal?' asked Stone.

'I'm sayin' it's as cold as charity outside, so I'd expect all the windows to be tight shut.' Murray pointed down the corridor. 'The room on the left, at the end. The window's wide open.'

'Then, let's git after him,' growled Stone.

They rushed back on to the balcony and clattered downstairs to the bar-room. On their way past the bar, the marshal collared one of the two bartenders.

'Go fetch Ben Brady,' he said. 'An' tell him, when he's dealt with the three corpses here, there's another needs pickin' up out at Ollie Prout's home-steadin'.'

The bartender nodded.

Meanwhile, Stone bounded across the bar-room ahead of the others and pushed open the batwing doors. As he did so, Leroy Cheney galloped past on a mettlesome black mare. Stone dashed outside, but, before he could bring his rifle to bear on the fleeing saloon-keeper, Cheney had vanished into the darkness in the direction of Ollie Prout's homestead.

The Kentuckian swore roundly, then pounded along the sidewalk towards the law office. Upon reaching it, he swiftly unhitched his gelding from the rail outside and leapt into the saddle. He thrust the Winchester into the saddle boot and set off in pursuit.

By the time he reached Ollie Prout's homestead, he had cut Cheney's lead to about half a mile. Stone urged the gelding on. They sped past first the homestead and then Kate's one-time horse ranch. The open plain lay ahead and two miles further on was the ravine through the mountains that the locals named Wolf Pass.

Leroy Cheney and his black mare

plunged into the mouth of this pass. By now the distance between quarry and pursuer had shortened to a little more than quarter of a mile. Glancing back over his shoulder, Cheney felt a tremor of fear run down his spine, while Stone, his face set in a look of grim determination, relentlessly and remorselessly cut down the gap between them. Both men sensed that the chase would soon be over, for Cheney's black mare was built for speed rather than stamina, whereas Stone's bay gelding could, it seemed, go on for ever.

Cheney glanced desperately to his left and to his right. But there was no escape. There was no break in the snow-covered walls of Wolf Pass. They stretched upwards, icy and perpendicular, to the snowbound rim of the ravine. Again he glanced back over his shoulder. Stone was nearer still, a mere hundred yards behind him now.

The saloon-keeper dragged the long-barrelled .30 calibre Colt free from the shoulder rig beneath his black Prince Albert coat. Turning in the saddle, he aimed the gun at the fast-approaching Kentuckian and fired. But it was the act of a despairing and panic-stricken man, for Stone was not yet within range of the revolver.

The sound of the shot echoed throughout Wolf Pass, to be followed moments later by an ominous rumble. Leroy Cheney was too intent on avoiding capture to take notice of this rumble and galloped on, deeper into the ravine. Stone, on the other hand, at once realized the danger threatening both of them. He swiftly pulled up the gelding, turned the horse's head and, wheeling round, galloped back the way he had come.

The saloon-keeper's shot had set off an avalanche. As the sound of the shot reverberated up and down the ravine, the towering piles of snow high up on the rim were suddenly loosened and came tumbling down, bringing with them the snow packed hard against the sides of Wolf Pass.

Two huge white blankets crashed

down into the pass, to form an inexorable, thunderous, unstoppable mass. Trees and shrubs were flattened. Everything that stood in the way of that gigantic moving white wall was buried beneath tons of snow.

Leroy Cheney understood too late his perilous position. He promptly turned round and spurred on the mare, riding hell for leather in the wake of his erstwhile pursuer. But he had retreated no further than fifty yards along the ravine floor when he was overtaken by the avalanche. Horse and rider disappeared beneath the white torrent.

Jack Stone was luckier. He had turned and fled in the nick of time. He emerged from the mouth of Wolf Pass only moments before the ravine was filled with snow to a height of fifteen or more feet. Indeed, the avalanche spilled over on to the plain beyond, almost, but not quite, engulfing the Kentuckian.

He eventually pulled up a few hundred yards from the pass and looked back. He had failed to apprehend Leroy

Cheney and take him back to Horse-shoe Bend to face justice. Yet he reckoned that justice had been served. He smiled wryly. It was ironic that, in the end, Cheney had brought about his own destruction. Stone turned in the saddle, dug his heels into the gelding's flanks and headed back towards town.

# 10

Christmas Eve dawned bright and sunny, and Horseshoe Bend awoke to the glad news that Leroy Cheney and the Inglis gang had ceased to rule the town and were either dead or in jail.

Consequently, Norman Black called together a meeting of the town council in the dining room of his hotel. There he was unanimously reinstated as mayor until an election could be held early in the New Year. The conduct of Marshal Bill Murray during Cheney's reign of terror was discussed and, while some council members criticized him, it was decided that, in the end, he had vindicated himself and should therefore remain in office. Several other matters to do with the business of running the town were then discussed, and it was as the mayor was about to call the meeting to a close that the Reverend Daniel

Dunwoody marched into the room.

'Good morning, gentlemen,' he greeted them. 'And it really *is* a good morning now that law and order have been restored.'

'Quite so, Daniel,' said Norman Black, while the others cried, 'Hear! Hear!' or simply nodded their agreement.

'I am sorry to interrupt your deliberations.'

'That's OK; we were about to adjourn,' replied the mayor.

'Well, I won't keep you long.'

'You carry on, Daniel. We ain't in no partickler hurry,' said Black.

'That's right. You say what you gotta say, Reverend,' added Sid Harrison.

'Very well. It's like this: I reckon the one person who has consistently stood up to Cheney and his cronies is young Kate Driscoll. 'Deed, she has put us all to shame.'

'Yeah, I'm sorry to say she has,' agreed Bob Stevenson, the blacksmith.

'And what did she get for her pains?' enquired the clergyman. 'I'll tell you. She lost all of her stock and her horse ranch ceased to exist.'

'That's so,' said Black.

'But it could be restocked.'

'Coyote ain't got the capital. She — ' began Harrison.

'Needs a loan, one which this town could easily provide,' Dunwoody finished the storekeeper's sentence for him. 'I suggest that we do just that, that we provide the wherewithal for Kate to restock the ranch. And I also suggest that it be an interest-free loan.'

'Wa'al, I dunno,' said the mayor hesitantly.

'This town needs a horse ranch. Its presence on the edge of town will help boost our prosperity. It will encourage folks from all over Moose County to come to Horseshoe Bend.'

'I s'pose.'

' 'Course it will, Norman. It has in the past.'

'OK. Say we grant Coyote this loan. How long do we give her to pay it back?'

'We don't set a time limit. You all

know what a fiercely independent person she is. She hates to be beholden to anyone. She'll pay off that loan just as soon as she possibly can, believe me.'

Norman Black carefully considered the pastor's words.

'You know, I reckon she will,' he said at last. Then, addressing the assembled council members, he demanded, 'What do we do, gentlemen? Do we grant Coyote this loan?'

'If'n she ain't too proud to accept it, I say we should,' declared Bob Stevenson.

'An' so do I,' said Sid Harrison.

The others, too, voiced their agreement and, when Norman Black called for a show of hands the motion to grant Kate Driscoll the loan was carried without dissent.

'Now all you've gotta do, Daniel, is persuade her to accept it,' said the mayor.

'I will,' said Dunwoody confidently.

And, without further ado, he left the hotel, climbed into his gig and rode out to the erstwhile and, he hoped, soon to be restocked horse ranch, where Kate greeted him warmly.

''Mornin', Reverend,' she cried. 'What brings you out here? I'd've thought, this bein' Christmas Eve, you'd be busy with church matters.'

'I shall be later,' he replied. 'But firstly I need to speak to you.'

'What have I done?' she asked warily.

'Nothing. It's what you are going to do,' he said, and he went on to inform her of the proposed loan, emphasizing how the resurrection of her horse ranch would benefit the town.

Kate, who was both proud and stubborn, was not easily persuaded, but Daniel Dunwoody persevered and eventually, after much hesitation, the girl agreed to accept the town council's loan.

'There is one other thing before I leave you,' he said. 'You are invited to supper tonight. And,' he added firmly, 'I shall not take no for an answer.'

Kate smiled shyly.

'Oh, that's kind of you!'

'We sit down at seven.'

'I won't be late.'

Nor was she.

Supper was a jolly affair. The food was excellent and the conversation lively and full of cheerful good humour. Everybody chipped in, including the two young Dunwoody children. Kate relaxed and thoroughly enjoyed herself. Having removed her battered Stetson and her long, scruffy coyote-skin coat, she presented a pretty picture despite the shapeless check shirt and baggy denims.

This had not escaped the notice of Pete Redford. Indeed, the Texan had difficulty in averting his gaze from the girl, a fact which Jack Stone observed with a smile.

The meal ended with Hannah serving the three men, Kate and herself coffee and the two children buttermilk. Then, once this had been consumed, Kate pushed back her chair and rose from the table.

'That was a lovely meal. Thank you

so much,' she said to Hannah and, turning to the pastor, she declared, 'I'd best be going home now, Reverend.'

'I had hoped, Kate, that you would stay and come to the midnight service with us,' said Dunwoody.

'Yes, you will be most welcome,' affirmed Hannah warmly.

'Oh, please do!' cried Paul and Ruth together.

Kate looked round the table at all the friendly, welcoming faces. She suddenly felt a great desire to do as they asked.

'But . . . but I cain't go dressed like this!' she exclaimed, peering in distress at her old, ill-fitting work-worn clothes.

'We are much the same height and size,' said Hannah. 'Come upstairs. I'll find you a dress to fit you.'

'Wa'al . . . '

'Please.'

Kate capitulated. And when, some-time later, the two women returned to the sitting room, Kate was neatly attired in one of Hannah's gingham dresses, with her short dark hair freshly brushed and her face pink and smiling.

'Gee, aren't you pretty, Miss Driscoll!' cried Ruth in astonishment.

'She ain't jest pretty,' remarked Pete Redford. 'She's downright beautiful!'

And to think that he had once mistaken her for a boy!

For Kate, that evening proved to be the happiest of her young life. She relished every minute of it. Then, sometime after the pastor had left to prepare for the service, it was the turn of the rest of them to walk across the street to the church. They went across in pairs. Hannah and Jack Stone walked arm-in-arm in front, then came the two children and lastly Kate and Pete Redford, also arm-in-arm.

As they approached the church doors, Redford said quietly, 'I guess you'll be needin' someone to help you run your hoss ranch once it's restocked?'

'Yes, I shall,' replied Kate.

'Wa'al, I'd like to be that feller,' he said.

'You! But I thought you were keen to

return home to Texas?' she murmured.

'I was. However, I've kinda gone off the idea. So, whaddya say?'

'Oh, yes, Pete! I'd like that very much.'

The young Texan gave her arm an affectionate squeeze and they entered the church, their faces flushed and wreathed in smiles.

By the time the service was due to start, the church was packed. Horseshoe Bend's escape from the thrall of Leroy Cheney and the Inglis gang had induced those citizens who did not usually attend this midnight service to come and give thanks to God.

The Reverend Daniel Dunwoody welcomed the congregation from the pulpit and announced the first hymn, 'Once in royal David's city'. This was sung lustily and with true fervour, as were those that followed. Dunwoody preached a splendidly uplifting sermon and the service concluded with the congregation singing joyfully, 'O come all ye faithful'.

Then, since it was by now Christmas

morning, the pastor wished each and every member of the congregation a merry Christmas as they trooped out of the church.

The last two to leave were Hannah and Jack Stone. And, after he had hugged and kissed his wife, Dunwoody turned and grasped the Kentuckian warmly by the hand.

'Merry Christmas, Jack,' he said, adding, 'And it is mainly thanks to you and young Pete that Horseshoe Bend is, after all, enjoying a season of peace and goodwill. Which, I must confess, is something I have long been praying for.'

'Wa'al, Daniel, your prayers have surely been answered. So, mebbe you could say God had a hand in it, too?' replied Stone.

'Yes, Jack. I should like to think so,' declared the pastor.

'Then, let's call it a small miracle,' said Stone.

*Other titles in the*
*Linford Western Library:*

# JUDGE COLT PRESIDES

## George J. Prescott

When one of the powerful Ducane family is hanged for murder in a border town, his father wipes out the place in revenge. Deputy Federal Marshal Fargo Reilly goes south to dispense justice and becomes involved in a gun-running conspiracy, and a plot to murder the president of Mexico. Reilly and his deputy Matt Crane fight to destroy the gang. But can Reilly also stop them from ransacking the nearby town of Perdition, where *Judge Colt Presides?*

# BLUEGRASS BOUNTY

## Jack Reason

The most wanted gunman and outlaw this side of the Rockies, Jude Lovell, is about to hang in the town of Saracen. The crowds flock to be at the event of the century. But Marshal Brand is deeply suspicious. Why are there so many of Lovell's gang gathered in the town? Have they come to mourn, or to stage a daring rescue? When the awful truth dawns it wreaks a devastating toll of death and destruction.

# KNIFE EDGE

## Tyler Hatch

Brad Winters, ramrod of the Block F ranch, only wants to do his job. However, his boss Matt Farrell has other ideas: he wants to re-enact the Battle of Hashknife Ridge, which had been fought there fifteen years earlier. It means a meeting of North and South — and old hatreds are far from buried. Before the battle begins there are shootings, robberies and assassination attempts. And by the time it's over, the wonder is that there is anybody left alive.

# ONCE A RANGER

## Hank J. Kirby

'Once a ranger, always a ranger' — so the saying went. But when Clint Taggart left under pressure, he was never happier. Then tragedy struck and the rangers wanted him back. Against his better judgement, he agreed and found his life and that of his remaining family in unimaginable danger: up against the biggest threat Texas had ever seen! But he still retained the old Ranger training, and Clint rode to meet his enemies head-on, determined to face the consequences.

# WARRICK'S BATTLE

## Terrell L. Bowers

Haunted by the past, Paul Warrick is assailed by bad memories, and in an attempt to forget, drifts from town to town finding work. But a shoot-out at a casino lands him in jail, and with the valley on the verge of a range war, Paul's actions might be the fire to light the fuse. Paul becomes involved in the final show-down — and he must not only save his life, but also his own sanity at the same time!

# MAN OF BLOOD

## Lee Lejeune

When he visits his brother, Texas Ranger Tom Flint finds Hank dying and his wife Abby abducted after an attack on their homestead. Soon Flint runs up against a gang of vicious layabouts working for Rodney Ravenshaw, who is trying to retrieve family property by underhand means. Can Flint live up to his Comanche name of Man of Blood and save his brother's homestead by ridding the town of Willow Creek of its nest of vipers?